Lillie Rebek

The Home of the Dragon

a Tonquinese idyll, told in seven chapters

Lillie Rebek

The Home of the Dragon
a Tonquinese idyll, told in seven chapters

ISBN/EAN: 9783337267681

Printed in Europe, USA, Canada, Australia, Japan

Cover: Foto ©Andreas Hilbeck / pixelio.de

More available books at **www.hansebooks.com**

ANNA CATHARINA

—

THE HOME OF THE DRAGON

A TONQUINESE IDYLL

TOLD IN SEVEN CHAPTERS

LONDON

T. FISHER UNWIN

PATERNOSTER SQUARE

—

M DCCC XCIII

To

MY HUSBAND.

CONTENTS.

INTRODUCTION.

IS there anything like the sunshine in the East? Anything like the sky, the sea, the people? Who that has been in the East can quite forget his first impressions?

Thirty-eight days, and I was cut adrift from all the prose of the old country—at least that is what I thought when I first put my foot on Tonquin soil, and breathed, with rapturous delight, the mystery-filled air of my new surroundings!

For the evening the cook had prepared a grand dinner. To be truthful, I was a little disappointed. It was not quite "*natif*" enough; I wanted everything "*au naturel*,"—for *natif* was my great word then, and I had before me indistinct visions of birdsnest soup and fermented eggs and chopsticks.

How well I remember this first meal. I can see the flowers in the centre of the table now —big yellow double marigolds and little pink roses laid out in fanciful pattern round a sugar-loaf shape. When I pulled one of the flowers out I found that it had no stem, but was stuck into a mould of river mud! The table was laid very correctly; the two house-boys stood near the dresser, looking very decorative in their white clothes and black turbans. I found that instead of a napkin I had a pillowslip under my bread. It was delightful, so deliciously unexpected.

Then, let me see, we had oxtail soup, then fish, and the boy had put two red hibiscus blossoms where once had been the eyes. Then a dish of wild ducks, and roast chicken and salad.

It does not seem entertaining to you, my gentle reader, this quoting of a menu? But with me it is different. Let me but smell the odour of one of these dishes, or see a big patch of sunshine on a whitewashed wall, or feel the fanning of some scented summer breeze, or hear the squeaking of a wheelbarrow, and I am back once more in yonder sunny clime.

Let me but smell, feel, hear one of these things to-day, and, quitting this chilly north, I roam about at large.

I first go back to the old house standing in the sunshine by the river. The green shutters are closed. I walk about on the verandah and wave my hand to our neighbour; the ribbons of her light wrapper are fluttering in the wind, but she cannot see me.

Then through space (for I despise the staircase) into the court. The dogs are all asleep: I cannot resist the temptation. "R-r-rats," I say. They send a frightful tremor through my body, for they run right into me, regardless of my feelings.

As I pass the kitchen my instincts as a housewife are very strong; I must just have a look. That man has never cleaned his cook-room for the last six months. The pot is boiling over, the bird by the fire is burning to cinders. Whatever is the cook doing? He is sitting in a chair, trying on a pair of pale blue silk stockings. They are mine, and I lost them years and years ago. I hunted everywhere, till I came to the conclusion that the cockroaches must have eaten them. I call him by his name; he does not hear. Ha! could I but materialise!

"Naï-ah," I call. The wretched cook-boy is playing in the sand outside the door instead of turning his spit. I pull his little dirty ear, but for all that they will have a burnt chicken for dinner at the white house.

Then to the garden. My flowers are all in bloom at once: hibiscuses, red, pink, and yellow; the rose bushes, the camellias, a dozen kind of lilies, the creepers, and, spreading shade over all, a Japanese lilac tree. I shake it, and the mauve petals fall in a scented shower. How I breathe their perfume! There flies a butterfly, more beautiful than a flower.

From a distance come sounds of tam-tams and gongs, pipes and flutes. It is a procession. I make a rush for the wall round the cisterns. The boys, the cook, the wretched Naï, my old amah, are already there. They talk excitedly, but I never knew a word of Annamite. I sit upon the wall, regardless of the broken glass.

Here they come. Three men have been found inspired in the Buddhist temple and they form the *pièce de résistance*. One is a Chinaman—he stands on a table carried by four men, the lance is thrust through his tongue which protrudes; the second man is an Annamite—he has the weapon pierced through the left cheek, and the pointed tip just shows through the right cheek; the third man is again a Chinaman, who mutilates his upper lip. They do not seem to suffer; but still it is a ghastly sight. The blood has dried round the wounds, and some of it lies in ugly spots upon their dusty everyday clothes. Their eyes are clouded like the eyes of opium smokers. There is a strange belief amongst the people. They say, that when the lance is taken out, the wound disappears without leaving a scar.

How I feast my eyes on the gorgeous colours! What silks, what embroideries, and all just thrown over the ordinary rags! What banners, what strange inscriptions! On they pass in an endless stream amidst the infernal noise of their hideous music. All the different temples send their fineries, their musicians, their lacquered chairs, that each respective spirit who takes part in the procession may rest from time to time. And then comes the big dragon.

Our pantomime dragon must be a brother of his. But this one is bigger, finer, more alive, with men inside who are fanatic acrobats. Wherever he passes, volleys of crackers are fired, and shrines erected in his honor.

How my people enjoy it on the wall! So absorbed are they, that when the monster lifts his head unexpectedly they fly back, and the fat old washing coolie tumbles into the cistern. I am furious and I tell him so. Why, he is spoiling our drinking water for the next six months.

Down comes the rain. Such a shower, drops as big as dollars, and they make a mighty noise as they fall. Nothing do I enjoy more than a real good downpour. I mean, too, to have a treat all to myself, for there is

not a soul stirring. I should
think every one was asleep yet.
All by myself is really not the
right expression. I must fetch
Hamlet.

Hamlet is a gander—a bright,
intelligent bird who came to us
as a baby. He was originally
meant for dinner, but when I
saw him in the kitchen, his poor
wings tied together, I thought I
had never seen such a pretty
little head. No, he was too
thin to roast, and he was put
into the farmyard to grow fat.
He thrived amazingly, but the
farmyard is a sham institution
and Hamlet was never eaten.

What a cackling there is
amongst them when it rains!
Thirty chicks, and as many more
ducks and peacocks and turkeys,
who are thoroughly enjoying
themselves. You may fancy
when I tell you that even the
heron grows communicative.

But I leave them to their
cackling; I only want Hamlet.
He knows it too. As soon as he

sees the door open just the tiniest little bit, he makes his neck as straight as a poker, opens his beak, flutters his wings, and makes for the gutter running round the house. There are great protruding spouts at the corners, and the water comes down in a clear fresh stream. Hamlet and I, we take a most delightful douche.

Sooner or later, of course, it was sure to happen. I mean to say, somebody or other would be sure to surprise us. And it did happen. And of all the people in the world, who do you think?

The governor-general! Our governor-general. Nothing could have been worse!

I had no stockings on; I had had some slippers, but Hamlet, that ridiculous bird, always pecked at them, so I had kicked them off, and they were lying in the path; my clothes had melted away to nothing. And then my hair, of course a douche is nothing with a bathing cap.

He came quite close. He
must be frightfully near-sighted,
else he would surely act as if he
had come the wrong way by
mistake.

I coughed. But remember it
is only a thought-body cough,
and they are not audible. He
walked straight through my
slippers, and, standing on my
toes, stroked Hamlet on the back
with his stick.

Or I can go back in the middle
of a typhoon and sit on an old
table which they have forgotten
in a corner of the verandah. The
white house by the river is shut
up, double barred all the windows
and doors. And so are all the
other houses and Annamite huts.
Frightful is the howling of the
wind; the whole building is
trembling to its very basement.
The air is filled with all sorts
of things: banana-trees, sand,
stones, loose leaves, bricks, cor-
rugated sheet-iron, the flowers
from the gardens, chimney-pots,

chairs—I know not what. The straw-covered houses are losing their roofs. The river is changed into a roaring sea.

An Annamite junk comes past. She has broken loose from her moorings. She is spinning round and round like a top, now the stern to windward, now the bow. The foam-tipped waves sweep her decks. For a moment I see an Annamite woman standing at the bow; she has a child in her arms. She makes some desperate signs, but her voice is lost in the storm. I shut my eyes in terror, and when I open them again, junk, woman, child, all have disappeared.

I, too, am going—at least my table is, and we are carried before the wind. Heigh ho! how we go. We fly away over the white house, and it has a big hole in the roof. I can look into the dining-room. On, on, till I come down in the paddy-fields. I put out my hand; yes, it is raining—a tiny misty close sort of rain. The typhoon has passed by.

Shall I buy a baby? It is an absurd idea, but it haunts me. It is because the Amah is sitting in the hall, and with her an old Annamite woman and a little chubby girl. My maid that was does not want to give fifteen dollars. She feels the little thing all over like we might a fowl for dinner. The old hag sticks to her price. Shall I say twenty-five, and bring her up with a bottle? But I cannot afford it.

Once more I must have a whole day in the country—there where I know of the dearest of little pagodas and the country all around so beautiful and the shade of the fine old trees so cool! I shall have a sort of picnic. I shall take the dogs, and must take a boy as a precaution against pirates, and take provisions for seven. There is first Filou and Folette and Scapeque and Maholen, and two pups which have not yet been christened. I am bound to take them, for without them Folette would not enjoy herself a bit, and she would cry real tears. No, I take them in a basket. Then there is myself, dear memory I.

How we enjoy ourselves! We have regular meals every two hours and games between. We visit the temple full of grinning, even-tempered images and red ancestral tablets, and all sorts of things of which I do not know the names or the meaning. Folette makes us believe that there are rats, but it turns out to be a lizard, and I will not have her eat these tiny, pretty, transparent things. I give her a banana in compensation. As soon as the sun goes down we go home, for I don't like pagodas in the dark. As we leave, an old beggar comes round the corner—a walking mummy without the swaddling clothes, instead a few coffee-

brown rags, a stick in one hand,
a much - battered hat in the
other. He has made a tray out
of his hat to receive the offerings
of his charitable brothers and
sisters : a miscellaneous collec-
tion of all sorts of things : some
cooked rice, a bit of dried fish,
quarter of a betel-nut, five small
coins, an old sardine tin, and
half a soda cracker.

Tam, tam, tam, all night, and
the miserable wailing of the cry-
women. There must be somebody dead somewhere. It is the
washing coolie's grandmother.
He has so often said that his
grandmother is dead, that when
he said so again yesterday, nobody would believe him. But
this time she is really dead, and
the washing coolie is chief
mourner, and to-morrow, the
day of the burial, he will walk
backwards in front of the seat of
the soul—a red lacquered chair—
and wear a coarse white gown,
and strew ashes on his head.

And some more sounds of

gongs and tam-tams. It comes across the fields ; I follow it and get into a village.

There is something going on there, for the whole population is gathered round their temple. The body of the building seems to be reserved for the members of one family. To the left, on a bench, is a pale Annamite. She must be very ill, for she is supported by two women and looks as if she might pass away any moment. A woman in a green silk dress is dancing in front of her. From time to time she uncovers a small looking-glass, rubs it with a silk cloth and peeps into it—an endless ceremony, and I ask in vain for an explanation.

And I will go and have dinner with Asaing; she is a comprador's wife. Asaing greets me with a smile of welcome. She is a tiny woman, and looks like a girl of sixteen. Still she is mother of a great big baby. Her face is daintily painted, her jacket is made of bright blue silk, and she wears ugly black drawers. Asaing has small feet, and hobbles about in a distressing manner. We are greatly interested one in the other, and we talk with our hands. I object to her diminutive shoes and her poor mutilated feet; she puzzles at our stays. Then we have dinner together, and the little woman is as happy as a child, and gives me the choicest bits.

But there are so many, many places I re-visit, and one seems ever dearer than the other. I must not weary you, my gentle reader, by taking you with me on all these wanderings.

There is still the Chinese street with its curiosity shops, and the whitewashed hospital where many of our brave soldiers have breathed their last; there is the evil-smelling market; that pretty court where our good sisters sit and work, and teach their little brown-faced waifs and strays how to hold a needle; the river alive with a hundred small crafts; there is the little church-yard where the hibiscuses are always blooming, and where the water stands a foot deep in the newly-dug grave; the truly Annamite towns up country, the verandah-girt homes of the French amidst their pretty gardens, and the wall warmed by the broiling sun where the coolies sit, men and women, chewing betel-nut. But enough, enough.

In latitude 20 N. lies the new French possession of Tonquin. It is a marvellous country, inhabited by a strange people, and I lived there for two years.

In the following pages I have made an attempt to describe something of what I heard and saw.

For a European woman it is very difficult to get an insight into purely native life. We get a glimpse here and there.

Sometimes the servants are truly attached to us, and they tell us of their domestic troubles,

which are many, and their plea-
sures, which are few.

We walk through their villages
and peep into the cottages, so
tiny and so full of people. Their
pagodas are our resting-places,
always in the prettiest spot of
the landscape—their cool hall
and their shady trees are precious
in this sunny land.

Their noisy rites penetrate to
our quiet homes: some one dead
or some one being buried, some
feast, some procession.

Then there are the days of the
Têt, the Annamite New Year.
For three days all native houses
are shut up, no work is done.
Fancy a whole country not at
home for outsiders for three
days! There is a child born
over the way—it is a boy and
great is the firing of crackers.
A wealthy Annamite may send
an invitation to come and see
his chrysanthemums in bloom.
Then we walk about in the
strangest of strange gardens, and
in a corner of his hall is his wife

and the children, all dressed in their very best. We shake hands all round, and try to solve the mysteries of our toilettes. The sampan on the river is a Chinese puzzle. Grandfather, grandmother, father, mother, three children, all live, sleep, eat, die in this bit of a boat, and a dog maybe and a cock in a basket. And withal they are as happy as sand-boys.

Then there is the Chinese meal with chopsticks, and with clumsy fingers and many fears we try to do justice to the complex culinary art of the celestials. And then there is the religion of this people, of which we see so much and know so little. The care for the aged is its main feature, also the care for the comforts of the dead, who continue to have material wants after death. The Annamite's solicitude for the white heads in his home is a beautiful phase in his domestic life.

I have tried to put some-

thing of the Eastern sunshine
into my story, but where the
light is very bright, we must
remember that the shadows are
deep.

THE HOME OF THE DRAGON.

—••—

THOSE FERNS.

TO lie on a Tonquin river in the month of August is a questionable treat. The sun is scorching, mosquitoes are plentiful, and at best the launch or gunboat, or whatever your craft may be, can be but small, and want of space means want of air.

I had an old sailing vessel, of Norwegian origin I think, for a temporary home. This old ship had been acquired for the purpose of transforming it into a floating godown; it had been towed up the river, and was then moored near the Hanoï customhouses.

All day I had been watching

the floating population surrounding us, and they were both varied and picturesque. Endless bamboo rafts had passed by, a hut in the centre raft giving shelter to several generations of lusty Annamites. There is always a baby and a yelping, black-tongued puppy, both tied to strings and fastened to the empty husk of a melon, so that in case they should tumble overboard their whereabouts might easily be ascertained.

I had done all that can be done on an old sailing vessel transformed into a godown, and that was not much. After having spent a whole day in inactivity I had the prospect of a lonely afternoon. So, it being four o'clock, I said to the coolie—

"Coolie, get the pousse-pousse ready and I will go for a drive."

Soon we were spinning along merrily. My coolie is a fine runner, and his legs are good to see. When we got to the *Rue des Bamboos* I had an inspiration.

"Coolie," I said, "we will go to the Pagode Balny."

He turned round and mopped his head.

"It is a long way, madam," he said.

"Oh, never mind, we have plenty of time."

So we turned back, crossed the town, and went round the lake. This Hanoï lake is very pretty. It is situated in the centre of the European town. The Government buildings are close, the embankments are well laid out, and there is a small island with a picturesque little pagoda and a few huts. Then on through endless native streets, which are animated and odoriferous. In the busiest parts of our busy European towns we have nothing like the life in these Eastern cities. One has but to go into their streets and look on to get a very fair idea of their ordinary mode of living. Everything is done out-of-doors—from the rejoicings over the birth of a

male child to the wailing over
the dead. All the houses are
open. There is the whole family
either at work or squatting round
the rice-pot and the dish of fish
or pork. The children are at
play in the street, dirty and un-
dressed; the little ones are pretty,
but as they grow older they become very plain.

We had soon left the town
behind us, and were coming
through pretty country roads.
When one comes from the delta
this country round about Hanoï
seems beautiful, but one must go
further into the interior to get
into really fine scenery. Still
the abundant green everywhere,
the softness of colouring, are a
surprise and delight.

After a good long drive we got
into a broad avenue. I left the
coolie in the shade of the pousse-
pousse, and walked on. I saw
that the avenue led up to a sort
of gateway, more or less dilapi-
dated, but effective. Through it
I walked into a wilderness of

trees, bushes, and bamboos.
Presently I saw to my right a
big lake. Shall I ever forget
the first sight of this water? I
don't think that there is really
anything very beautiful about it,
and I cannot exactly explain
either wherein lies the charm.

There is a sort of little tank
walled off from the lake, railings
run round the top of the wall,
and some steps lead up to the
shore. I suppose this reservoir
must have something to do with
the pagoda which stands on the
left side of the road. I scrambled
up and sat on the top of these
railings, my feet dangling the
while over the wall and the
water of the lake under them,
my back to the road. There I
sat and sat and thought of all
the fairy tales that had ever
been told me in my life.

Nowhere could I see the shore.
Big trees with their branches
lying on the water made the
most beautiful bordering. The
lake was covered with aquatic

vegetation. The lotus were not yet in flower, but countless heavy buds, with their pink petals just bursting the green leaves, were appearing above the surface. Wherever the water was visible it was dark and liquid. On the leaves sat here and there a paddy bird, and ever and again I saw the blue wings of a kingfisher bent on business. All this to myself. Glorious !

I thought of the good folks at home, and their going here and there and everywhere to get away for a time from the smoke of civilisation. But where could they go? Well, say Norway. But did not Jane tell me in her last letter that when they came to Dröntje, a tiny fishing village unmentioned by guide - books, they were greeted by a hideous monster advertisement in their own native tongue, and, to quote Jane, "After that we did not feel ourselves justified in walking down the village street without our gloves " ?

No, this was the place for
them. Here was I, a woman,
living at the end of the nine-
teenth century, back in Paradise.
Not a soul to interfere between
me and nature, and I had but to
look around to feel that to be
was in itself a gift of the gods.

In the tank and round the
edge of the lake there grew a
lovely fern. Having come to
the end of my contemplations I
resolved to gather some, take
some plants of it home, and see
whether I could make them
grow. But let me try to describe
it, as I never saw one like it before and have never met with it
since. Let me remark that I
know little of botany.

To begin with, this fern has a
long, slender stem, or stems, and
they lie on the water and the
mud, the leaves shoot out of
them in all directions, and are
like ordinary feathery fern leaves.
The strange part is that the new
leaves grow out of the old ones,
and other ones again out of

these, till there is a perfect net-
work of them, and their trails are
yards long.

I saw that the best ones were
right in the water, so to facilitate
operations I took off my shoes
and stockings, hung them over
the balustrade, and, tucking up
my skirts and my sleeves, I went
fern-fishing with a will. The
roots grew deep in the river mud,
and had to be pulled out very
carefully so as not to damage
them. I worked till I had collected quite a little pile. I filled
my handkerchief with river mud
so as to help their acclimatisa-
tion on my verandah, and then I
went into the road and stowed
them carefully away in the
pousse-pousse.

I remembered then that I had
come to see the pagoda, and if I
wanted to get home before night
I had better do so at once. The
pagoda does not outwardly differ
much from those distributed in
great numbers all over the
country. It is neither big nor

very beautiful. There are first some three or four broad stone steps, then a paved court of small dimensions. The building is low, the roof curls up at the corners in the fantastic style of the ornamentation of the country. There is a narrow coloured pottery frieze running round the inside edge of the roof. There are some fine hard wood pillars, and some carvings over the porch. The door is a heavy double one. There are the mellow tints of antiquity about the place, wherein, with its utter stillness, lies its greatest charm.

I tried the door; it was open. On each side was a sort of little alcove, and within each of these niches stood a big wooden horse —an exact copy of a Nüremberg toy; there was the identical colouring, white with red-brown spots. I have no idea what they were there for, and what their meaning. Above them was a small square window.

Then through another porch I

entered a good-sized hall. I stood in presence of a big bronze statue of Buddha. His round face wore the smile of good-nature and simplicity. His large hands rested on his knees, the long-nailed fingers spread out stiffly. Round the side walls sat numerous statues of saints; some were golden, some lac-quered red, and all wore the same sweet smile of superior goodness. There was but one barred window in the back wall, and through it came all the light.

I was just preparing to go when the door shut with a great noise. I jumped with fright, for in the great stillness I was quite unprepared for any sound. I ran to the door. It was shut. I listened. There was certainly nobody outside. I used all my strength to lift the latch. The door stirred not. I called; no answer. In a moment I was filled with terrible forebodings. I remembered suddenly where

I was. This was the Pagode Balny, where but a few months ago a young brave French officer and his men had been surprised and been put to horrible deaths.

The betel-nut stains on the floor had quite another meaning to me now—they might be blood for all I knew. I looked round in an agony of fear, quite expecting to see some hideous faces in those little windows. I hardly dared to move.

Did I say that Buddha had a nice face? It wore the ugliest of sly smiles. And as for those dumb, wood-carved squatters, they seemed to contemplate my terrors with fiendish satisfaction. How terribly real they grew too! Why, the nasty things were alive; their very shadows sent thrills of fright to my soul. I did not dare to scream for fear of detaching one of them from their pedestals, and making them do something atrocious and unexpected.

But it was absurd to go on

like this. I began to reason
with myself. I said, " It is the
wind. Of course the wind shut
the door. Very well, supposing
it is the wind, how am I to get
out if the door is shut and I cannot open it? If I must sleep
with these frightful idols I shall
go crazy. Of course the coolie
will miss me, he will come and
look for me." Nothing of the
kind. He will snore till to-
morrow morning. I did not
remember having seen him
awake except at meals or when
running. I was sure he was
sleeping that very moment, and
to put an end to these arguments
with myself I laid my fingers on
my ears, shut my eyes, and
began to call with all my might.
But there was no answer.

I was all but on the verge of
giving way to despair when I
remembered the windows above
the horses. Could I possibly
get through them? they looked
so very, very small. How I re-
gretted my daily and prolonged

banana feasts between lunch and
dinner! If I squeezed hard I
might get through, and even if I
got but half it was better thus
than stopping in this ghastly
company.

With spirits revived I climbed
my horse as if he were an ele-
phant, that is to say, by the tail.
Once well on his back it was
comparatively easy to get at the
window. I managed to unfasten
the shutters, and oh! delight, I
could just get through it.

I was sitting on the sill, the
greater part of myself once more
free members of society, when,
to help me in my gymnastics,
my left foot must have given the
poor horse too vigorous a kick,
for with a great noise I heard it
turn over behind me. In another
second I was on the ground, and
did not I run! I never stopped
till I had my hand on the coolie's
shoulder. He, as I had antici-
pated, was sleeping peacefully in
the shade of the tree, and had
neither heard nor seen anything.

" Home," I said.

As we made our way through the darkening country I had time for reflection. I did not think I would visit lonely pagodas again without a proper escort.

As we came nearer to civilisation, that is to say, nearer to the lake, I saw to my dismay that I was minus my shoes and stockings. I had left them on the balustrade.

" Coolie," I said, " go home by the back streets," and I thought of Jane and her gloves in Dröntje village.

The next morning, before the sun was too hot, I went to the pottery street to get something to plant my ferns in. After I had searched awhile, I found some terra-cotta boxes which seemed made for the purpose. They were about a foot and half in length and rather narrower in width. On all sides there were holes of the size of a shilling piece. I acquired a dozen, and

took them on board, and at once
set to work to plant my ferns.

That same evening I returned
to my home, and on our verandah
the ferns thrived amazingly.
They soon covered the whole
boxes and overhung the balus-
trades in long, graceful trails.
They were a constant source
of pleasure—my first thought in
the morning, my last care at
night. But my poor ferns were
to come to a tragic end. And
this is how it happened :

When they were in the very
height of their beauty I had to
absent myself from home and
leave them in the care of the
houseboy and coolie. I was long
before I came to the conclusion
that it was utterly impossible for
me to take twelve boxes of ferns
to a friend's house. So I had
the boy and the coolie up on the
verandah, and there, in presence
of my precious ferns, I told them
what they had to do, and they
promised faithful obedience.

When I had been a week with

my friend I began to worry about
my ferns.

"Linda," I said, "I am sure
they won't look to those ferns at
home. I wish I——"

"Do you know that you are a
perfect nuisance with those ferns?
Boy, go and tell the steam-launch
to wait; madam is going home."

"I won't be long, dear; just
the time to have a look round,
and I shall be back for dinner."

A very bad sign. When I came
home, as I entered the hall, I saw
both boy and coolie armed with
water-pots, making a wild rush
for the verandah. I did the same.

My poor ferns were dead—
stone dead, shrivelled, scorched,
petrified, done for—the mud one
solid brick in each of the twelve
boxes. And there were my
faithful servants pouring water
on them by the ton, and under
my very nose, too, muttering all
the time to themselves that they
loved me very dearly.

"Boy," said I, "go and fetch
a stick."

He did so.

"There. Now give the coolie five strokes."

But the coolie did not make the necessary preparations. He had something on his mind—that was plain. Presently he chin-chinned in humble and approved fashion.

"Madam," he said, with the face of a gravedigger, "when the coolie has had his licking, where shall he put the unlucky boxes?"

"The what?"

"The boxes, which are un-lucky."

"What is the matter with the boxes? They are very nice."

"Yes, madam, they are *beau-coup jolie*, but they are unlucky. The ferns must die in these boxes. Madam sees, they are dead, quite dead. These are bad boxes; they are for the dead ones, the ones born dead, the dead born little ones. The mistress understands that the boxes are not good."

Poor old coolie! I had un-

wittingly made flower-pots out
of children's coffins. Was it a
wonder the ferns withered?

Greatly relieved to find that
nobody was responsible for the
untimely end of my ferns, I went
back to the other side of the
river. I found that I had just
time to get ready for dinner.
Near my plate lay a brown paper
parcel addressed to me in an unknown hand.

When I opened it I found a
pair of much-battered shoes and
stockings, in which I recognised
my long-lost property. Mechani-
cally I passed my hand up one of
the hose.

"No," said Linda, "no holes."

Yes, heaven be blessed, they
were neatly darned. Who sent
them?

The mystery has been left un-
solved to this day.

A-QUAÏ'S WEDDING.

AN old woman is squatting by a charcoal fire in a little earthenware stove on which there simmers the refreshing potion which is presently to bring strength and healing to her suffering mistress. There is no light, only the reddish glow from the burning embers. But dimly does it light the small square apartment. There is a door with carved panels and red joss-papers. This door leads into a narrow court. Now, it being evening, the bamboo poles are fastened. Outside swings the red lantern, throwing an unsteady glimmer on the pavement below.

In one corner, pasted to the wall, a gaudy painting of the household god on red paper dotted with gold, a black table underneath covered with a red cloth embroidered with blue and white silks, dragons, and some pewter vessels. One is filled with sand and holds the joss-sticks. Slowly consumed by a sleepy little flame, they fill the room with sickly odour and send forth long trails of smoke. It hangs about in mid-air and gathers in a small blue cloud under the ceiling. There are two wooden benches, a few bamboo stools, and a round table in the middle. A stair in one corner leads to the room above. There is no window.

Thimooä, the old woman, squats by the fire. She looks like a heap of different shades of brown, from coffee-brown to dull terra-cotta. Her clothes hang about her in untidy folds, her naked feet are wrinkled. She has hidden her head on her knees, and is hugging her legs with her arms. From time to time she lifts her head and listens. It is the face of a very old woman, brown and full of wrinkles; the hair is grey and coarse, the eyes are dim, the lips are red from the juice of the betel-nut.

Thimooä lifts her head and listens. Now and then sounds reach her ear from the chamber above. It is weary, weary waiting.

A-Chook's hour has come. A-Chook is the compradore's wife, her young mistress. Oh, the long, long night!

A wailing sound comes through the stillness, and with it a new one, the one so long expected.

"Thimooä, hasten thee; bring the warm clothes and the drink. It is a boy." This from the wise woman, a bulky Chinese matron, whose head appears at the head of the stairs. "Hasten thee to the master and tell him a boy has been born."

Thimooä reaches up the clothes

4

and the drink, and, unfastening
one of the bamboo poles, she
slips out into the court that
runs between the two high walls.
A little further along the wall
there is a door similar to the one
just unfastened. Thimooä enters
an apartment much the same as
the one she has left, only one
side is partitioned off by wooden
planks, and with gay hangings
forms a spacious sleeping-place.
The curtains are drawn, and
there is a faint odour of opium.

"Master, awake. The mis-
tress sends Thimooä to say that
a boy has been born."

The old woman's entry has
awakened the sleeper, a man of
middle age, thin, pale, and well-
featured.

"The mistress sends Thimooä
to say it is a boy."

A gleam of pleasure comes
into the dreamy eyes. His first
wife has borne him no children,
and A-Chook is his second
wife, and therefore the boy is
welcome.

"When thy mistress can let
me see her, I will come."

"Yes, master."

The baby grew into a boy—a
big boy. When he was twelve
months old his mother, who was
a tiny woman, could not carry
him any longer.

"I think I must get a girl to
carry me the boy, he is so big.
Besides, he wants to play and be
out."

The friend who had come to
participate in the good things
set forth on the occasion of the
firstborn's festival was of her
opinion.

"Yes, thou art right; he is a
big boy. It breaks thy back to
be for ever carrying him."

Thimooä overheard this conversation.

"Mistress, Thimooä knows of
a maiden who would suit thee."

"Hold thy hasty tongue, old
mother. If thou wert good for
anything thou couldst carry him
thyself, but thou art too old, and

the boy loathes thy ugly face and dirty clothes."

"Good mistress, this maiden I think of would suit the boy. She is young and comely and of good parents. The master could have her cheap. Ten dollars— that would be nothing for so fine a girl."

"Ten dollars? Why, for an unwashed Annamite? Didst thou say ten dollars? Be gone, old mother!"

The rebuke mattered little, for, as events showed, Thimooä's words were spoken at a good time. It was but a few days later. "Thimooä," said the mistress, "what about this girl? Who is her mother? Didst thou say ten dollars? It is a goodly sum —too much for an Annamite girl. I will again speak to the master."

The outcome of this conversation was that, towards the end of the week, Thimooä was pushing a little Annamite girl up the stairs and into the presence of the mistress.

" Mistress, here is the child."

Mother and baby looked with curious and critical eyes at the new acquisition. After a good stare they fell to handling her clothes, which were miserably poor and scanty, her hair, her hands. The child kept close to Thimooä, the old woman, and from time to time sent up an anxious look into her face; but Thimooä's face said nothing; there was no answer to the child's pleading eyes.

"There, take the boy. Canst thou carry him? Dost thou like her, son?"

The little maid smiled, and with a clever movement she sat the heavy baby astride on her back and tied him fast in the shoulder-bag. She was proud to show her strength. The boy pulled down her handkerchief, and the long black hair fell over her shoulders down to her bare brown feet.

"She will do, mistress. If thou wilt be patient with her

for a day, thou wilt see what a good bargain it is."

At the end of the day the mistress gave Thimooä ten dollars in silver pieces.

"What is the child's name, mother?"

"Let the mistress name her."

"All names are good. Let it be A-Quaï."

Little A-Quaï is asleep on one of the wooden benches in the lower room. Her knees are drawn up, her head lies flat on the wood. She has but scanty coverings. The child's breathing is soft and regular. All is quiet, for the household is gone to sleep. Old Thimooä is putting in the poles and shutting the door for the night.

As she comes in she draws her flimsy garments closer round her spare form. Passing the little sleeper, she listens for a while and looks around, then going softly to the other bench, she undoes the bundle that lies under it, and takes out a spare garment.

She lays it gently over the child, and bends her head till the warm breath touches her old cheeks.

It has been little A-Quaï's first day of servitude. The Annamite does not love the Chinese, and only the very poorest of the poor serve in their households. What does the old woman think of as she looks at the child asleep, tired out by the heavy baby? Does she think of the little maid who has done with childhood, or does she think of the ten dollars that lie in a little hard lump secure in her waistband?

Thimooä's face is not expressive, and presently she rolls herself up on the other bench and goes to sleep.

Little A-Quaï is quite at home in her new surroundings. She wears the blue jacket and the black, ugly trousers of a Chinese girl, her long hair hangs in a plait down her back, and finishes off with a heavy red silk tassel. She carries the boy on her back, and when they get into disgrace A-Quaï takes the whipping without flinching. "Old mother," she will say in the evening, "it did not hurt."

She has two friends. One is Gang, the Annamite office-boy, the other is A-Chee, the Chinese cook. When Gang buys the flowers which the old flower-coolie brings in the morning for the mistress's head-dress, he keeps one for A-Quaï. The child puts it behind her ear, and the baby says that she is pretty. Gang thinks the same.

A-Chee, the cook, gives her cakes and dainties. When she saw the cook for the first time, little A-Quaï thought she would not like him. He had a smooth face and an ugly mouth, and its smile was incomprehensible to the child. But did he not give her cakes and good things ? And being but young, she said, " A-Chee, the cook, is my friend."

So little A-Quaï grew into big A-Quaï, and the baby into a good-sized boy. She became maid to the mistress, for she was clever with her needle. Now one day something happened that was to bring great changes into A-Quaï's life. And this is how it came to pass.

A-Quaï had gone into the kitchen with a wooden pail to fetch hot water for her mistress's ablutions, for it was fast getting dark, and the evening meal was finished.

The cook was smoking his pipe. He was leaning against the kitchen door, and watched her, with a smile, while she was pouring the water into the bucket. She was preparing to take up her pail when she noticed that the cook had left his position at the door and was standing in front of her.

"Come, A-Chee, make me not lose my time; let me pass. The water is getting cold, and the mistress will scold."

A-Chee looked at the girl with his ugly smile. The girl was pressing up closely to the wall and shaking off the hand which was trying to take possession of her arm.

"A-Quaï," said the cook, " don't be silly. I will not hurt thee ; but I am fond of thee, and——"

" Say but one other word, or touch me with thy dirty fingers, and I will scream and bring the mistress here. Let me pass."

" A-Chee, thou son of a pig, let the girl go ! "

It was Gang, the office-boy, who had come to the kitchen with the same purpose as A-Quaï. He sprang forward, and, with a mighty shake from behind, he set the girl free.

A-Quaï was breathless with fear and emotion ; her hair undone, her garments disordered, her face white with terror. The two men eyed each other in silence.

" Touch him not, Gang,"

said the girl, bringing forth each
word with an effort, and laying
her hand on the young fellow's
arm; "he is a heap of dirt."

But her words were of no
avail. Bursting forth into a
volley of furious abuse, he flung
himself upon the other man, and
they fought like madmen.

Somehow this encounter came
to the ears of the mistress in a
somewhat changed version. The
cook had a clever tongue, and
he had so twisted the story that
A-Quaï and Gang had been
represented as the offenders.

"A-Quaï, thou shalt have a
beating, and a good one. Thimooä, get the stick."

The mistress, vexed at the
girl's silence, had thus ordered a
severe and humiliating punish-
ment.

All that day A-Chee, the
cook, lingered about the court to
get a glimpse of A-Quaï. She
was now standing at the door,
pale and sad.

"Say but a word," he whispered, as he caught sight of her, "and I will save thee this licking."

"Begone, son of a pig! I mind not this licking. See, there is Thimooä, the old woman, and she has got the stick." She looked with a bitter smile at the slender reed.

Without a word the two women enter the room, the girl takes off her jacket, and lies flat on the ground. The old woman proceeds to administer the promised chastisement. The girl lies quite motionless. At each stroke she draws her breath in sharply.

The old woman looks old, very old. Her face says nothing.

Poor old Thimooä. Poor old mother!

The night has come, people have gone to bed. From a distance sounds the gong of the watchman. The poles are fixed in the door. There is only the dim light from the joss-sticks.

It is very quiet in the little chamber. A-Quaï, on her bench, cries softly to herself. The old woman rises noiselessly and goes to her, and puts her wrinkled cheek against the girl's wet face.

" Oh, grandmother! "

" Daughter of my daughter. I who love thee! They made me do it. I am old; what can I do? "

" Let us go away. Oh, grandmother! Come, we will go. Come now, arise, and we will be gone when the morning comes."

The girl is sitting upright, and is looking earnestly at her grandmother.

" I will put on some of your clothes, and we will be gone. Oh, come, grandmother, come! "

She crept to the other bench and pulled out the bundle of nondescript garments which formed the old woman's wardrobe. She dresses in nervous haste.

" Come, we must not lose a

minute.   I will not stay.
Come ! ''

The girl half pushes, half
drags the old woman along, and
once outside the door they creep
along the dark side of the court,
then across the quagmire behind
the buildings, and to the river,
where they hail a sampan, and
cross to the opposite shore.
They walk all the night.   When
the dawn brings the fresh morning breeze they stop.

" Come, mother, we will rest
here ; but we must not sleep.
Where didst thou say the village
was ? ''

The old woman pointed in the
direction of the sea.   " There,
child, it will take us all the day
to reach it.''

Thimooä looks very old.   The
excitement of the last few hours
has left her weak and worn.
A-Quaï looks at her anxiously.

" Mother, eat ; thou must not
fail now.   Thinkest thou they
will help us in the village ? ''

" They will know me ; they
will give us food and shelter.''

"Come, then, mother. We must walk on. Lean on me."

So they trudge through the hot morning, the shadeless afternoon. They have no more food, they are hungry and weary, and walk in silence. Old Thimooä's step becomes slow and dragging; she leans heavily on the girl.

"Seest thou yonder tree, child? There we will rest. I can walk no more."

The sea lies like a silvery band in the distance.

"Oh, mother, bear up a while longer. There are the rocks. We will sit on the top of them and feel the breeze. It will refresh thee, and thou shalt rest, and I will go to the village and get food. Come, mother!"

The girl runs on in front. Her feet are touching the first soft sand of the broad beach. Here and there a rock stands out black and craggy, for it is low tide.

The girl shades her eyes with her brown hands, and looks up

and down the beach. Yes, at a
small distance she can see the
fishing village, well hidden by the
bamboo hedges.   The village
where Thimooä, the old woman,
was born, and her mother and
she, A-Quaï.

Poverty had driven the old
woman to town to look for work
in a Chinese household.   She
had lost all her children, both
sons and daughters.   Little A-
Quaï was the one left to her old
age.

When the child's mother had
sickened she had said to the
dying woman, " Fear not, I will
care for thy little one.   Is she
not all that is left to the old
woman ? "

She gave the little girl in
charge of a neighbour, went to
town, and sent regularly the
two silver coins that were her
monthly wage. When A-Quaï
grew into a girl she longed to
have her near herself, and could
think of no better way than to
bring her into the same house-

hold and offer her to her mistress.
A-Chook was a good-natured
woman, and the money would
be kept to go back one day to
the child. In good time her
mistress would give her in marriage, and she, Thimooä, could die
in peace. She kept her relation-
ship to the child a secret, so
that in time she might be thought
worthy of a good match.

A-Quaï stood shading her
eyes, and drank in the fresh salt
breeze, and listened to the waves
as they lashed the beach and the
rocks. A sudden noise made her
turn round.

"Oh, mother! What is it?"

There was no answer. The
old woman had stumbled and
fallen forward on her face, and
lay now quite still. A-Quaï's
face grew ghastly with terror.
Was this death? Was the
mother dead? The child shook
her gently, and turned her over
on her side.

How terribly thin she was,
how sunken the eyes, how

wrinkled the face, the hands, the feet !

The child was speechless; she knelt down by the rigid form and watched her in an agony of fear.

From time to time she called, "Grandmother! Oh, grandmother!" But there was no answer.

The heavy tears fell one by one on old Thimooä's clothes and on the brown stuff; they looked like big, black spots.

"I thought so. Here they are !"

The girl has sprung to her feet, and looks like one who sees a ghost.

"A-Chee, is it thee ?"

"Yes, pretty one, my jessamine blossom, flower of delight. I followed thee, and see, I guessed right."

In her terrible sorrow the child had not noticed the figure of a Chinaman coming towards her at a running speed across the beach. She only saw him when he had spoken to her, and then he was standing quite close to her.

A-Quaï looked round wildly.

" No, it is no use. Thou wouldst run away? I can run faster than thee. Come with me. I love thee, flower of delight! Look, there behind those rocks thou wilt see the steam-launch. I told the master, ' I know where to find them.' But I see thou canst not see it from here. We are on the sands, but the tide is coming in, and we will soon be afloat."

The girl looked at the man with fear and loathing.

"I will not leave my grand-mother; she is asleep. No, I will not stir. Touch me not!"

" The old woman is dead. Come, girl; if thou wilt not go of thy own free will, I will carry thee."

He laid his hand roughly on the girl's arm.

" Nay, let me be. I will go."

With a set face and a resolute

step the girl walks in the direction of the launch. A ship's boat takes them alongside. On deck they are greeted by a deafening clamour of voices.

It is all great fun to the crew. Two women trapped like mice. The one dead, the other alive! Oh, jessamine blossom!

"Give me to eat; I am hungry."

The girl speaks in a harsh, faint voice.

"Yes; let her come. Sit down with us. Here, here, here! It is a wedding feast. The meal is ready. Come, boys, let her sit here. Oh, the flower of delight!"

"Listen, you sons of pigs. Listen, you dirty ones. If you but touch me with your grimy hands, I will throw myself into the sea, and my spirit shall come back and give you no peace. Leave me alone. Give me to eat."

The men laughed uncomfortably, and went to take their evening meal.

A-Chee brought her a basin of rice. The girl eats in hungry haste; then she sits down near the bow and looks towards the small brown patch on the light sands.

The launch began to move. A-Quaï buried her head in her lap and cried.

"Now listen, girl. I have been good to thee, and I will even now forgive. But mark me, this time thou shalt not run away. Thou art a woman, and thou shalt be married. To-morrow thou shalt be married. I will give thee thy wedding clothes. They shall be handsome, pink silk, and the first one shall be green. Thy hair shall be dressed by A-Chingha in the butterfly pattern, and with a new style of flowers. Thy shoes shall be lavender, embroidered in gold. Thou shalt have a scented hand-kerchief. Thou wilt be a pretty bride. He offered eighty dollars. It is much money for a coolie's daughter. But the master has a kind heart. He says, "Let A-Quaï have half of it, and it shall be her master's wedding present. I think A-Chee——"

"Didst thou say A-Chee, mistress? Didst thou say A-Chee, the cook, shall be my husband? Oh, mistress, have pity! I loathe him. Hast thou not seen his ugly face? It is fat and flushed. He drinks wine; he will beat me. The painted women take his money. Oh, mistress, I loved thy little boy so well. I love thee, mistress. I will work for two. Let not this man be my husband. Take not his money."

"It is the master's doing, child. It is all settled. Thou hast disgraced thyself. It is time thou shouldst be married. Be not foolish: one is as good as another. When we saw thy foolish flight this morning we did not know where to find thee. Gang, the boy, knew nothing. A-Chee said, 'Let the master lend me the

steam-launch, and at nightfall
I will bring back the two women.'
He has kept his promise. Be
reasonable and make the best of
it. Go to bed now."

When, at nightfall, A-Quaï
had been brought home in
triumph, she had been taken
upstairs into her mistress's room,
and the cook had explained the
details of her rescue. Was it
the fact of the girl coming back
alone or the tale of anguish
written on the young face? The
mistress abstained from harsh
words, and when the cook had
left them she spoke to the girl
of the marriage which had been
arranged during her absence.

"Come, go to bed, and to-
morrow thou wilt think differently."

A-Quaï went in silence, and
laid down on her accustomed
resting-place. The lonely chamber
and the empty couch brought
back her sorrow with renewed
violence.

Gong! gong! went the beat of

the watchman, and each time
the dogs burst forth into dismal
howls. A-Quaï thought of her
old grandmother on the sands.

Had she been asleep? Had
she been dreaming? There it
was again—the same small noise.
There must be somebody at the
door. What could it be? Without a sound she crept to the door
and listened.

"A-Quaï, A-Quaï! It is I—
Gang. Art thou there? Art
thou listening?"

"Yes, yes."

"Mark what I say. Fear
nothing. To-morrow, in the
cook's chamber, under the bed,
thou wilt find clothes. Put them
on. There is a window; jump
out. I will be there. Dost thou
listen?"

"Yes, yes."

"Then go to sleep. The dogs
are barking; I must go."

Oh! jessamine blossom, where
are all thy sorrows?

The morrow has come.

"That is right," says the mistress, who watches the butterfly glory slowly taking shape out of A-Quaï's abundant black hair. "Be joyful. A bride should do her weeping alone. I am glad to see thee without thy tears. They would spoil the white and carmine. Thou art beautiful. But A-Chee has been a faithful servant these many years; it is but right that he should have a pretty bride. I should put just a little more red near the eyes. There, that will do."

The mistress and the two women that have come to complete the bride's toilette chatter merrily. A-Quaï heeds them not; she has her own thoughts. But when they make her look into the glass her little heart gives a great thud of pleasure to see herself so fair and winning.

She has been ready in all her gorgeous finery for quite two hours, and sits quite motionless on a stool not to crease her silks or disarrange the elaborate and *perplexe* edifice of the butterfly glory.

"Come, now; it is dark."

They put the beaded crown over her head, and, supported on each side by one of the women, A-Quaï is taken into a sedan chair and carried before the cook-house. The cook has a room above the kitchen, and under firing of crackers and beating of gongs the bride goes through her ceremonies. The women lead her upstairs, and leave her there to presently greet her husband, who is now feasting with his friends.

The women are gone. A-Quaï listens to the creaking of the stairs, and waits till she hears them cross the court; then she bolts the door. She looks under the bed; there is the bundle. She trembles with excitement. She undoes her Chinese finery, gets into the Annamite clothes, pulls off her crown, the flowers, and wraps a kerchief round her

head. Then she goes to the
window, unfastens the shutters,
swings from the sill for a second,
and disappears into the darkness.

THE RENDEZ-VOUS.

I.

THERE was a great bustle of furbishing and scrubbing on board the *Bémoll*—great spring cleaning, in fact, if such a term will still hold good for the last day in October. The *Bémoll* is a fine old man-o'-war, or was once, for at the time of this story she is the headquarters of Commandant Vernon and his staff. The *Bémoll* was taken out to Tonquin as a troop-ship, and at the completion of her voyage steamed up to the shore, and the stokers drew her fires for the last time. She dropped her anchors and let down her gangways. All the machinery was taken out and replaced by comfortable quarters for the men, and everybody thought the good ship had done with navigation. Not quite, though.

Once there came a typhoon and changed the placid river into a great sea, and when the good people looked out in the morning after the storm the *Bémoll* was gone. The spectators smiled, for somebody said she must be in the paddy-fields. They got their glasses and scanned the horizon, but there was not the smallest speck to indicate her whereabouts. Near midday a rumour ran through the town that something was being towed up the river. Could it be the *Bémoll?* Two tugboats, and in their rear the *Bémoll* herself. By sundown she was secured to her old moorings, looking much as usual.

When the Commandant and the officers went to take their after-dinner cup of *café noir* at the restaurant they had a hard time of it. The jokes were weak and plentiful. Also did the good citizens think this expedition and happy home-coming a fit occasion for general rejoicings, and there was merry-making and *Veuve Cliquot* till the stopping of the punkahs and the snoring of the punkah coolies reminded them that it wanted but a few hours to dawn.

But of course all this has nothing to do with the present story, and, as has been said before, there was spring cleaning on this special day, great furbishing, scrubbing, and splashing of waters. The men with their bare feet and uncovered breasts worked away with a will. The officers in charge, with their caps pushed well back on their heads, ran backwards and forwards, and every now and then they took out the long-view telescope to see whether the flag-mast at the harbour-master's had hoisted the black ball.

Round the stern of the *Bémoll* there runs a gallery, on which is room for two or three easy-chairs, also a small table or two. This gallery is protected by a white railing; a board runs round the outside, forming a rest for flower-pots with ferns, crotons, camellias, and hibiscus. These flowers are Commandant Vernon's pride. He has watered them at all hours of the day and the night, and is at this moment bending over them with his water-can to give them their refreshing draught after the heat of the day. He is a middle-sized man, of about sixty years, with a kind face and rather commonplace but pleasing features. The eyes are good, brown and bright. The hair is cut quite short; it is grey and white at the temples; a very short, neat moustache.

He has finished watering the flowers. From the gallery, through one of the windows, for there are two, you enter the saloon, which looks restful and comfortable with its warm red hangings and white and gold paint; there is a table in the centre, a sideboard opposite to windows and gallery, and doors to the right and left.

The Commandant lifts the curtain that hides one of the doors to the left and enters a good-sized cabin. There is a happy smile on his face as he looks approvingly around the white abode. It had been his idea that it should be all white, and after the painters had done their work he had set himself to combining and arranging, and certainly the result was satisfactory. There stood the dainty bed with its mosquito curtain and a big white bow to tie it up with. He is shaking the folds into better shape and remaking this bow, over which he has already spent the best part of the morning. There is a white toilet table, wicker chairs, and flowers in a stand. In a corner the crucifix and a painting of the

Holy Virgin kissing her babe.
The evening sun sends her last
rays through the open portholes
and fills the cabin with golden
light. With a pleased nod to his
surroundings the Commandant
hurries off to disappear for a few
moments behind the door opposite ; then, in all the splendour
of full dress, he hurries on deck,
where he is greeted by one of the
officers with the good news that
the black ball has just been
hoisted.

The mail-boat is slowly steaming up the river, and as she
passes the French residence she
fires a salute and dips her flag.
Vernon is in the boat, and a few
strong pulls send him down the
river. Five minutes later he
pushes his way up the gangway
and on deck, where, with a little
cry of happiness, he takes possession of one of the lady passengers.

II.

When Marie Daule married
Commandant Vernon people in

general, and her people in par-
ticular, were pleased. Madame
Daule was a widow, and had
five daughters, and when there is
but a small portion to give to each,
this means a large family. Still,
four of the girls had been married very satisfactorily. Marie,
though not the youngest, had
tarried over her choice. The fact
is that Marie was absent-minded
and fond of painting, and, as
her mother said, was quite unconscious of possible suitors.

Commandant Vernon had
known the Daule family for years.
He had seen the girls grow into
women, and marked their suc-
cessive stages of development
by his regular home-comings.
He generally spent his leave at
Milan, and the girls loved him
dearly, and thought there was
nobody like their Commandant.
But he, he loved Marie best, the
pale-faced child, the bright-eyed
girl, the gentle woman. Marie
was now twenty-five years old,
but neither her sisters' teasing

nor her mother's gentle re-
minders seemed to impress the
girl with the advisability of
making her choice and marrying.

"Marie," said her mother one
day, "what dost thou think of
Commandant Vernon?"

The girl was mixing up her
colours, and listened but with
one ear.

"Think of him? What for?"

"Think of him? Well, I
mean dost thou like him?"

"Like him? Why, *bonne
mère*, yes, of course I do."

"Do leave those colours for a
moment, child. Listen, Marie.
He wants to marry thee."

The girl looked up quickly,
and broke out into a laugh, irre-
sistible and catching, and presently the mother joined in, spite
of the angry shaking of her
head.

"There is nothing to laugh
about. Only thou art so absent-
minded, and never see anything.
Speak, like a good daughter.
Say, wouldst thou like it?"

"I think I should, for he is the dearest of men. But, mother, I am so young, and——"

"That is all nonsense; I know no better man. He adores thee, only thou art such a little night-cap, and see nothing. He is strong and robust, and thou hast always been much older than thy years. I think you were made for one another."

Marie did not know, but *bonne mère* did, and as to the Commandant, of course she loved him. Why, she had loved him all her young days. So they were married and happy.

When the Commandant got his order for Tonquin he left a very sorrowful woman. Things were too unsettled in the new colony, and officers had no permission to take their wives; but before his two years were quite up things changed somewhat, and Vernon wrote home to Marie to come out by next mail if possible, and spend the last month or two with him, and see something of this new, wonderful possession.

Marie burst forth in songs of jubilation, cleaned her brushes and packed her paints, and, her young heart full of glad anticipations, she wended her way, *viâ* Marseilles, to the land of sunshine and bananas.

And here she was.

III.

Dinner for two. Vernon sits opposite his Marie like one in a dream. He can hardly take off his dear old honest eyes from the precious little person. Marie is above middle height, slim, with narrow hands and feet, a pale, oval face, dark brown hair, and liquid eyes. When Marie does not smile hers is a grave, pathetic little face.

"*Chérie*, thou dost look so well, and I could look at thee for ever. Thou art more beautiful than ever."

Marie takes everything seri-

ously ; some people say she has
no sense of humour, but that is
because they do not understand.

Marie is dissecting an oyster.
" Yes, Jean, I am well.   I am
happy that thou shouldst think
me beautiful."

Leaving the oyster alone, she
looks critically and lovingly at
her husband.

" Thou art none the worse for
thy campaign, my good one.
I have so longed to be with thee.
Now that I am here we will be
so happy.   I have made some
sketches, but one gets so lazy
on board, and then everything
is so interesting, one has not
time for anything."

When the sailor in waiting
has cleared the table they go
out on the gallery, and Marie
smells the flowers and looks
across the river, alive with many
a dancing light, and listens to
the new sounds.   Then they sit
hand in hand, Vernon unfolding
his plans for the coming weeks :
how they will rest to-morrow and

unpack, and go to the dance at
the Residence the day after, and
how they will in a few days go
to Along Bay, and up the rivers,
and how Dr. Borne is to join
them.

The following day Marie makes
a tour of inspection round her
new, strange, floating home, and
makes acquaintance with the
staff. The officers being young
and lonely, from that day hence
spend a good deal of their time
in personal adornment and wor-
ship at a distance.

IV.

The hospital is a long, low,
whitewashed building; a verandah, supported by square pillars,
runs all around it. The windows,
provided with green shutters,
open into this verandah. One
enters through a sort of vestibule,
and goes straight through a
long ward, where there are beds
in single file on each side, each
bed provided with a punkah. At

the other end is the doctor's
sanctuary. The walls are bare
but for a crucifix and a book-
case with books and instru-
ments.

The windows are open, and
the warm rays of the setting sun
lie in golden patches on the red
brick floor, the walls, and the
white bed-coverings. There are
not many patients, for it is
November, and the best time
of the year. A sister sits knitting, she talks to one of the
patients, and every now and then
sends a look through the open
door to the doctor who is writing
at his desk.

"It is half-past six, and he
thinks of nothing," she mutters
to herself.

Presently she gets up, and with
a determined shake of her great
white cap she picks up her ball
and appears before the writer,
who looks up with a smile and
strokes his bare chin in a dreamy,
absent manner.

"Is it that Monsieur le

Docteur has no idea what the time is?" she says, severely.

La Sœur Agnès is a tall, plain, gawky woman, and stands before the great man, reproach in her very attitude. The doctor still looks at her, fingering his chin.

"Oh, no, I am not laughing. You are too provoking. But I mean to be firm to-day. You shall go to that dance. Do you not realise that it is for the benefit of our poor sick ones, and that you, at least, must be there? But I will take you there myself."

"Do," says the provoking doctor.

"You are mocking me, but it is of no use. I shall not stir from here till you are gone." And so saying she makes a great clatter with her knitting pins and gives her cap a final shake.

"No, no, my sister; there, be not angry. See, I am going." The doctor gets up with a stretch, and goes across the gravel path that separates the hospital from his quarters. The good sister looks after him with a pleased smile.

He hated dances; not for other people, but for himself. Such a bother to dress. And then the ladies. He had no small talk; he could not remember what was going on in the town. Lobster salad at one in the morning gave him indigestion. White kid gloves made him wholly and intensely miserable.

Nevertheless half an hour later Dr. Borne is making, with many others, his way through the hall and up the stairs into the dancing hall of the Grand Hotel. There is a little knot of men near the entrance, watching the ladies as they arrive one by one. As each star appears on the horizon there is a little flutter amongst their special satellites. There are only about two dozen ladies in Haiphong, and dancing men must be quick and enterprising if they want to see their names on one of the programmes. Dr. Borne evidently does not participate in this excitement, for he is peacefully contemplating the decorations.

There are all the flags, sent from the navy and army stores for the occasion. They are hung in tasteful patterns over the walls. There are flowers and foliage in profusion, and big pink lilies and lotus buds, white blossoms which load the air with heavy scents, and hibiscus which brighten with their glorious tints the darkened corners. It is a big hall, full of light, and here and there amongst the green are bright frocks and happy faces full of joyful anticipations.

" Is it you, Borne, my good one ? "

" It is I, my Commandant."

" Come, let me introduce you to Madame Vernon."

Borne is a bashful man, and he blushes like a little girl or a very young man as he makes his bow to Marie. Marie is

wonderfully sweet in her white
garments that lie around her in
shining folds. Marie knows all
about the doctor : that he is
the son of a widow, and that he
has worked for her and a delicate
sister ever since he drew a
salary, that he is a hero in his
hospital, and that, altogether, he
is a good, great man. And,
above all, he is her husband's
friend. So Marie looks up with
a smile of greeting.

"No, I only dance square
dances," answers Marie to his
inquiry. Dr. Borne asks for the
favour of one. He does not
know himself why he does so,
only on seeing Marie he thinks
it would be good to dance too.
They dance together, and their
set at the quadrille raises a great
cry, for they talk to one another
and create hopeless confusion.
Marie lifts her grave face and
says, "It is very wrong of you
and me to dance when we do
it so badly. Come, we will
talk." Presently the Comman-

dant joins them, and they discuss
their trip to the Along Bay and
up the river. Dr. Borne is going
to join them, as his empty hospital will give him the oppor-
tunity for a much-needed holiday
He is fond of water-colours, so
is the Commandant and Marie.
They will start the next day.
The evening wears on, Marie
makes a few acquaintances, has
two or three more dances, and,
leaving the merrymakers, they
wend their way back home long
before dawn has set the cocks
a-crowing.

V.

The Along Bay is a wonderful
place. It is a place where Doré
should go with his sketch-book.
For miles and miles a wilderness
of rocks and sea, sea and rocks.
The sea is green, deep, and
transparent, and the rocks are
grey, rugged, of all shapes and
sizes, rising straight and uncompromising. When the tide

is low these silent giants are
wonderful to behold. The waves
have worn them into the queerest
shapes, and with imagination for
their godmother, they have been
endowed with a fanciful set of
names. There is never a sound
in Along Bay.

A small white steam-launch
is slowly zig-zagging her way
between the rocks. The evening
sun paints patches of yellow on
her white awnings and a golden
top to her mast. Marie, the
Commandant, and the doctor
are sitting at the bow. They
are silent.

"Jean," says Marie, "it is
very beautiful, but it is sad."

"Yes," says the Commandant,
"it is the region of eternal
silence."

"And of the oyster," chirped
in the doctor. "We will have
some for breakfast to-morrow.
You will see the sampans
come round first thing in the
morning."

It was a glorious evening; a

grand sunset, the sea and sky
and the rocks all ablaze in tints
of orange and violet. What a
place Along Bay is for evening
talk! Just when the sky is
losing its lights, and the night
is there before the sun has dipped
into the sea! They talked in
whispers, for their voices seemed
to go far across the silent waters.

Ah! the glorious awakening
in Along Bay! Marie rubbed
her eyes and peeped through
her cabin window. Oh, shame
to have slept when all things are
so beautiful! She got into her
slippers, and threw over her a
wrapper, and joined the two men,
who were quietly enjoying the
fresh morning air. Bay d'Along
in the month of November! It
is a dream. Some poet should
go there and sing its praises in
verse.

"There is not a vestige of
romance in you two men," said
Marie, as they puffed at their
cigars, heedless of the beauties
around them.

" *Voici* the oysters," said the Commandant.

A frail bark, through which the water leaks constantly and has to be bailed out with the carcass of a big old crab, pulls up, and for a trifle the fisherman empties the whole contents of his craft on the deck. These oysters are small, irregular, but so delicious. What a breakfast! Bread, butter, a bottle of Sauterne, and oysters—Along Bay oysters. That also is a dream.

Everything is a dream. All has become unreal—at least Marie thinks so. Something is weaving a strange spell around her. Something that was not there before has come. It is a new perception. There is disproportionate pain and bliss in small things. Where is yesterday? How long is to-day?

The blindness of the day before is gone. Marie can see. So can Monsieur le Docteur. And, *hélas!* they see but one the other.

VI.

It is long after the day in Along Bay—quite three weeks. The lauch is lying up some river. The travellers are on shore in search for sketching material. There is an old pagoda on the outskirts of a village, a pagoda built round a paved court on three sides. There are some flat tombstones and some big shady trees and a jessamine shrub. It is a lovely place, and it is the pagoda of many sorrows.

Marie sits on one of the flat stones; the doctor on another, the sketch-books by his side. The Commandant is gone to see whether the master of the launch is getting steam up, for this is the day fixed for the return to Haiphong.

The two sit in silence. They look up simultaneously. It came to them differently—to Marie with a great wave of pain, to

7

Borne with an incomprehensible thrill of bliss.

"Oh, Marie!" he whispers, jumping to his feet.

"Scht! for the love of God. I did not know it. Say not a word!" pleads Marie, breathing hard and stretching out her hands as if to ward off the possible approach of the man who looks at her in a wrapt ecstasy of love. She puts her hands over her face for a moment, and then, looking towards the river, she says, "Come, let us go."

Borne looks at the white face and the trembling lips. How sweet the woman seems to him —how dear!

"I am a brute," he murmurs to himself; "and he, poor devil, is my best friend."

"Come. Fear nothing." He took up the sketch-books, and silently they went on board.

Half an hour later the launch is briskly steaming down the river. The blue mist lies on the banks, and the water-birds are looking for their night-quarters.

"It is not Sunday every day," remarks the commandant, "and to-morrow we shall have to work."

When they sight the *Bémoll* the harbour is bright with lights. They wish one another good-night at the gangway, and it is only when Marie comes into the full light of the lamp in the saloon that her husband notices the white face.

"Why, my dear one, what ails thee?"

"Jean," she says, with a trembling voice, "I am glad we are back—so glad. I will go to bed."

"Why, little one, thou art crying. I have not given it a thought. Go and rest. No, do not kiss my hand, sweet one; your lips. I will bring thee something to drink."

So the eyes that were blind can see. Oh, pagoda of many sorrows! But what is to become of this wisdom gathered

in that one sweet moment
amongst the tombstones of departed Annamites? Marie does
not know, and for three long,
wretched weeks she wonders
and puzzles.

It was after one of the Resident's dinners that Borne said
to Marie, "If I meet you to-
morrow, when you go for your
ride, will you let me come with
you?" "You can come," Marie
had said, without lifting her eyes.

The whole night the woman
listens to the beatings of her
heart; but Marie is young, and
this is her first sweet love. And
then the miserable, endless day!

Towards sunset she rides her
pony down the narrow path that
leads across the paddy-fields into
the high-road beyond. There is
not a soul near. The new rice
shows its pale-green tips above
the water; the paddy-birds stand
out in dainty silhouettes; a lazy
buffalo with a crow on his back
is lifting his broad nose towards
the evening breeze. A flat land-

scape, with a bluish range of hills in the distance, a handful of huts with a hedge of bamboos around. Marie halts her pony; she sits quite motionless.

It is a strange thing. She has not been able to think at all since that promise last night. But now she can, and it has all become clear to her in a moment. Borne must never find her there—never, never! Good God, where were her senses!

With a desperate grip she turns round the pony, and back they fly at a mad pace. Marie does not look back nor stop till she reaches the bridge that connects the *Bémoll* to the shore. She runs up the gangway and through the saloon on to the gallery beyond, and, breathless and exhausted, she throws herself into an arm-chair.

The Commandant is peacefully reading his papers, a cup of tea by his side, his feet on the railing. " I will get you some fresh water. The tea is cold." He gets up to ring the bell. Clash falls something on the floor. He looks round sharply. Marie has laid her head on to the table and has upset the tea-things. She is sobbing bitterly.

He is by her side, stroking her hair that lies in wet masses around her forehead. A bewildered expression is on his face, his honest eyes are full of alarm.

" Jean," says Marie, " if I was to——"

A confession trembles on her lips. But no, she cannot, must not speak. It would kill this man. She must keep this to herself and be true if she cannot be happy.

" It is a sunstroke," says Jean, puzzled at this strange scene.

" It is the pagoda of many sorrows," thinks Marie.

VII.

Where the path that leads across the paddy-fields meets the road there stands a horse with a rider. The horse tries to keep off the flies with his tail. The man has taken off his cap, and from time to time he wipes his forehead. He gazes eagerly in the direction of the footpath across the fields. His very soul is in his eyes. But there is nobody coming; and with a wretched feeling of despair he knows within his heart that Marie -- his Marie — will not come, not that night nor any other.

He waits till all the light has faded out of the sky and the quick tropical night is creeping across the fields, then slowly, slowly he turns his horse and disappears into the darkness.

THIBA.

I.

IT was Sunday morning. The harbour looked lovely: the bright blue sky, the glittering river, the misty shores and far-off hills, the smart gunboats with their flags dipping into the water, and a soft, balmy breeze. I had, as was my custom on Sunday mornings, arranged the flowers in their stands and collected a fragrant bunch for the breakfast-table. The boy had let the blinds down, and I was enjoying the coolness in the central hall. I had a book, but did not read. It was too nice to do anything, so I sat looking at the cat, who was quite as lazy as myself.

It was ten a.m., and the gentlemen would not be in to breakfast till eleven, for the offices were only shut in the afternoon.

Why, of course this was Sunday; how time goes, to be sure! Thiba's day again. Poor Thiba! They ought to be here by this time. Poor little Peter and Marie! I was getting fond of those children, chubby little brown mortals. They liked me, too—or was it cupboard love? Of course there were the oranges and bananas, also sweets and cakes, also the tin soldiers for Peter and the doll for Marie; but never mind, I will not stay to analyse: I am fond of those children.

There was uncle coming up the stairs; he stepped heavily and looked to be deep in thought; he had an open letter in his hand. As he came nearer I saw that something had happened— something he did not like. His face looked cloudy, he sat down, pushed back his cap as was his wont, and scratched his head.

"What *diable* am I to do, I wonder?"

"Whatever is the matter?" I suggested, my sleepiness a thing of the past.

"Well, imagine my daughter, here is a letter from Férin. He has married, and is coming out by next mail."

"Why, but Thiba, his wife?" I said.

"No, child, not his wife."

I understood, and the newly-acquired knowledge made me feel miserable. I felt hot, and presently I could see my nose-tip grow white and pinched. My uncle was looking at me in an embarrassed way.

"Yes, child, such is life. The poor girl!" he said, folding his arms over his breast. "What can I possibly do? The next mail is due on Friday; and this is Sunday. Férin says" (here he took up the letter and read):

" ' DEAR MR. SIMON,—This mail
will bring you a *lettre de faire part*.
I am a married man of two years'
standing. I hoped to be able to
stay at home for some time, but
you know what the proverb says.
The long and the short of it is that
I have to be in Tonquin by the
17th of August, and, *hélas !* business is business. My dear wife
wishes to accompany me, and,
all being well, I intend to take
her. It is my wish that Thiba
should be informed of the step I
have taken. The allowance will
be continued as in the past. I
further wish to buy her a house
in N——, where she could live
in comfort and have the oppor-
tunity of well educating her
children, if she so wishes. My
dear, good Simon, be a friend in
need to me ; you have played
that part before. Arrange things
to the best of your understand-
ing, for old friendship's sake."
" Etc., etc.," said my uncle, and
looked angry. " No, I don't
like this ; it is a bad business.

Thiba is not like the other Annamite girls. She is a good woman; she adores her children, and, *hélas! la pouvre enfant*, she loves the man." We were both silent and busy with our own thoughts.

I remember so well. The first Sunday morning I had spent in Tonquin had been just such a one as the one described in the beginning of my story. At about ten o'clock my uncle Simon had come up, leading by the hand a little girl of two summers, and following came Thiba and small Peter. Thiba was an Annamite woman, tall and slender. Her face was more oval than is usual, neither were her cheek-bones so prominent. Dark, earnest eyes, but the beauty of the face was in the smile. The mouth was big, it is true, but a smile opened it gently, slowly, giving you a glimpse at the loveliest of teeth. Yes, such a smile — childlike, fresh, and catching; if Thiba had had nothing but this smile it would have been enough to impress you in her favour. But Thiba had many charms—a pale, soft skin, delicate hands, slender feet, black hair neatly parted down the middle, then twisted into a dark purple silk cloth and rolled round the head in turban fashion. She was dressed in the ordinary clothes of a woman of some means. A neat, dark, silk garment, slightly opened at the neck, displaying a necklace of golden beads. The under garments are of contrasting colours: say bright green and white, or perhaps red and orange, so creating a most pleasing effect. The garments descend almost to her feet, and, being split on both sides, the black silk ample drawers are left visible. With all that a white straw hat of fabulous dimensions, and little shining slippers turned up at their toes. Quaint clothes, to be sure, but Thiba was suited to them or *vice versâ*.

"Here is Thiba," said my

uncle, "Férin's wife. And this here," lifting the little maid on to the hall table, "is Mademoiselle Marie; and here," pulling forward the little fellow who was hiding behind his mother, "is Monsieur Pierre." My uncle was a grey old bachelor, and had the most chivalrous and gentlest of manners towards women, and he worshipped children.

Thiba and I looked at each other in outspoken curiosity, then she smiled one of her pretty smiles, and we were friends. The children were very funny. Peter was a true little Annamite, brown, fat, broad-faced, small-eyed. The little girl was a gem. She had some of her mother's refined beauty—in a baby way, of course—and a pair of liquid grey eyes. Yes, grey eyes; and somehow I always think when poor Férin shall have to answer for his shortcomings these two orbs will stand heavily against him.

I went into the dining-room

and came back with those things dear to the childish Annamite heart — bananas, oranges, and sweets. "*Merci*, Madame." This from Peter, who was a well-brought-up boy, and played the part of a man in a European sailor suit and hat. The babe on the table ate, and did the talking with her eyes.

" I shall leave the children with you for awhile if they are no inconvenience. Thiba likes to look at the harbour from the verandah."

And with a bright nod to the children Uncle Simon left us to ourselves. So it came to pass that every Sunday morning Thiba and the children had come to spend an hour with me.

Thiba was but a child in many ways, but her motherhood and the love she bore to her husband gave her a quiet dignity. Férin was the father of these children. He had been an old Tonquin resident, and he was a man of good family, but without means.

He had, therefore, worked hard; the road to prosperity had been long, but at last the reward of patience came. Férin made money, had a good deal of property in land, bought and sold, built himself a pretty house, cultivated a garden, and took unto himself Thiba. Thiba kept his house clean, brought in flowers and made the bare rooms pretty, and admonished the boys. In the course of time Peter and Marie were born, and the little household was happy enough. But even here the evil day came.

Férin got restless, home-sick ; he had not seen his people for these many years. His parents were getting old, there were his brothers and sisters, all married and with families; it would be nice to see them again. His little native town, too, and the haunts of his boyhood ; yes, it would be good once more to walk the old roads. So he said to Thiba : " What if I went to France the mail after this one ?

Ma foi, I want to see my country again."

Now Thiba had guessed the workings of her master's mind, and when she heard him say this she knew in her heart that he had already decided to go. Still the decision startled her. " Oh, Monsieur and the children and Thiba ? "

" Thou must stay here, my daughter, or take that house in N——, and I shall make such arrangements as will leave you and your children without care. "*Allons, ne pleure pas*," with a pat on her cheeks, " I shall come back, you know."

Thiba's eyes had filled with quick tears, her face looked drawn, and her voice betrayed her great emotion.

" Poor Thiba!" the girl said softly to herself.

The following two weeks went by quickly. Trunks had to be packed; the house was stripped of curios, useful for presents ; and then came the day that brought

8

in the mail. Thiba was in tears,
and went about like one in a
dream. The day of separation
had come. Férin would go to an
unknown land, to which even her
imagination could not follow him.
The dreaded separation had come.
It was there. Thiba was alone.
Oh, he was gone; he was gone!

Before parting Férin had said
to Thiba, "Every Sunday morning thou wilt take the children
and go to Mr. Simon. He is my
good friend, I have made arrangements with him. He will
take care of thee. If thou art
in trouble he will help Thiba.
Allons, ma fille, soie raisonnable."

Thiba had made an effort and
kept her tears for the darkness.
But one evening when Férin had
come to seek her in the garden,
she had asked him not to leave
Thiba and the children. "Thiba
loves you. Take Thiba and
the children."

" Thou knowest, my dear one,
I cannot do this. Be wise. I
wish dearly to see my old parents.

Thou wouldst not that thy little ones should leave thee in thy old age? No; be brave, and I shall come back." And so he did.

Thiba came to see us with the children every Sunday morning; sorrowfully at first, but as the time went by her face grew brighter, and she began to talk of the time when Monsieur would come back.

Uncle Simon and I sat thinking; I dare say our thoughts ran pretty nearly in the same direction. "*Que diable* am I to do? How am I to tell Thiba? Thiba is not like the rest of these Annamite girls. Money? Why, money won't do it."

I was beginning to feel something like abhorrence for this Férin. The vile man! I hoped I should never see him. I knew very well most of these Annamite girls were poor creatures indeed, but there were exceptions, and Thiba was one.

"Férin wishes her to take a house in N——. I shall never

forgive Férin; no! But he says I am his friend, so I must do my best. When Thiba comes, take care of the children, and I will tell her somehow."

Uncle Simon looked the picture of unhappiness. I knew well how his kindly, honest heart shrank from inflicting this pain. Presently there was a great to-do in the hall, and a " Down Follette!" from the head boy to the dogs, and a patter of small feet on the stairs. Here was Thiba.

When I came back presently from the verandah with the children Uncle Simon was gone. Thiba looked up oddly. Her face was pale and her lips trembled. I went to her and laid my hands on hers! " Poor Thiba!" I said. *" Moi beaucoup aimer Monsieur."* I think I had half expected a violent scene; her simple sorrow moved me deeply. This poor child; after her country's custom there had been nothing blamable in her relations to this man.

Her love was true and sincere.
She had been a faithful wife and
a loving mother. I did not know
what to say; Thiba was silent
too.

"Think things over," I said,
"and I will come to see thee
to-morrow night."

She nodded assent, took the
children, and went.

The next day after sundown I
rowed across the river to see
Thiba. She had put the children
to bed, and was sitting in the
garden. "Madame, be seated.
Madame is very good to come to
see Thiba." Then we talked for
some time. Yes, she would go
to N——, but to her mother's
home. No, not to this other
house; she did not care to have
it. No, she did not want the
money. Yes, some for Pierre;
he should go to school and learn,
for he was a Frenchman. She
would not take anything from
the house, the things were
Monsieur's. She would pack
her belongings and go. She

seemed quite cool and collected;
still she could not quite conceal
her sorrow and some of the
bitterness too. Of course she
could express her feelings but in
a very incomplete way, as her
French resembled in many ways
a child's talk. She seemed quite
to understand that she was
henceforth nothing in Férin's
life, and that the children were
hers only.

Two days after our talk in the
garden Thiba came once more
to the house. She brought the
keys. "You will find everything
in order. There is one coolie in
charge, and he will water the
flowers and feed the fowls."

The girl evidently meant to
keep strictly to business to the
exclusion of sentiment. Her
face was not in accordance with
her words though, for the
moment she looked at me her
eyes filled with tears. I put my
arms round her neck. She was
sobbing as if her heart would
break. "Thiba shall die."

"No, no, my daughter, thou
hast thy children. Be quiet.
In a little time thou wilt be
happier."

She shook her head sorrowfully,
and went slowly down the stairs.
By the evening Thiba and her
children were gone.

II.

Five o'clock in the afternoon,
and it is still very hot. The
blinds are down, giving to the
spacious room an air of coolness
which in reality it does not
possess. Two little fair-haired
girls in airy attire lie coiled up
on a long chair fast asleep.
Toddy, the terrier at their feet,
takes it easy too, and so, ap-
parently does Mrs. Lund. The
fan has dropped out of her hand,
and, quite regardless of the buz-
zing mosquitoes, she is indulging
in an impromptu nap.

"Bow-wow!" says Toddy, but
looks up at the same time; and
Toddy knows she has made a

great mistake, for Toddy, little fox terrier, are you and I not sworn friends? Of course we are.

It is a great pity to disturb this drowsy company, so I make signs to Toddy to keep quiet and we settle down on the most comfortable chair to follow the general example. But the chair is wicker and makes a hideous noise and creates instant commotion amongst the sleepers.

"Gracious, child! where do you come from?" This from Mrs. Lund with a wild stare.

"I thought you never slept in the afternoon."

"Nor do I. There, don't be disagreeable. It is so hot." With a groan and a stretch. "Look at the chicks; their hair is wet with perspiration. I can certainly not undress them any more. But why you do not get sunstroke, running about as you do, I cannot conceive."

"The thickness of my cranium," I venture to suggest, mildly.

"Pooh, that is nonsense. Take off your things like a good girl and get a "kimahno" in the bath-room. It makes me hot to look at you."

"Oh, I am all right. I must be up and doing. This heat is dreadful. If I keep quiet any length of time I shall dissolve and there will be nothing left to posterity but a grease spot. See?"

"Well, as long as you do not make me do anything I don't mind. As for the grease spot, that's not original. What did you come for?"

"Talk, of course. Also tea, also dinner, if you like."

Mrs. Lund gave a low whistle, which was one of her peculiarities. "Frieda, go and tell the cook Jeanne is going to have dinner with us. No, you had better tell him to come and speak to mamma."

Frieda got into her slippers and went on her errand.

"Have you seen her?"

"Whom? Mrs. Férin? No, I have not."

"Then I won't say a word. Wait and see. You know, though I don't like to say so, Mr. Férin looks like a nice man. I suppose his face is what you would call weak."

"What do you know about weak faces? Your brilliant imagination. It is simply because you have dabbled in his *passé*, and wept over that Annamite girl. No, don't be sentimental. Men are all alike."

I only smiled for answer. This was a way Mrs. Lund had of calling things by their right name. She called it taking the nonsense out of my romantic head.

Here was the cook. He chinchinned me in approved style, and then told us that there was soup, fish, ragout of ox-tail, roast chicken, and salad for dinner.

"Why, thou lazy one, we have had the same every day of the week. Throw away the chick,

and burn me that tail. Go and
get something number one for
dinner."

Cook was all smiles and promised wonders.

"Do you know that it is half-
past five ? And here, to be sure,
is somebody coming ! "

We made for the dressing-room
with a wild rush. I helped Mrs.
Lund into her clothes and presently the boy handed in two
cards—" Mr. and Mrs. Férin."
"Talk of the —— you know."
And to the amah, " I shall not
be a minute."

In the drawing-room we found
our new-comers. New people
in H—— are an event. We like
them, because they give us
something fresh to talk about.
Mr. Férin was a man of about
fifty, tall and rather good-looking, and his eyes were soft and
gray. Mrs. Férin was young,
say twenty-two, middle-sized and
slight, not pretty, but somehow
you seemed not to notice this.
Her eyes were good, and the cor-

ners of her mouth turned up a
little and made the face look
sweet and winning. She, of
course, was still in the first
enthusiasm experienced by all
travellers coming to the East for
the first time. Everything was
delightful. Her quaint house,
the garden, the river, the servants, the food, all and everything. Somehow I felt not quite
at ease with Mr. Férin; his secret
seemed to be mine more than
his. Or was it a secret at all?

When the visitors were gone
Mrs. Lund remarked: "I
wonder whether Mrs. Férin
knows anything?"

"I think she must know," it
seemed to me.

"That is because you are
romantic. Depend on it, she
knows nothing. He loves this
woman. No, he has not said
anything. But she will not live
long in this place without being
enlightened."

But this time my wise friend
was not altogether right in her

conjectures. For twelve months the Férin's lived happily and contented. Férin in his former residence in Tonquin had not been invited, as a rule, to the houses which boasted of a mistress. When he came back from Europe, bringing a young wife, things somewhat changed in his favour. The ladies were inclined to be friendly, and Mrs. Férin was asked to dances and dinners.

Things go by opposites in this life. I felt embarrassed with Mr. Férin, and Ninette was confidential and friendly. She was a pleasant, clever companion, and withal simple and open-hearted. I loved her very dearly by the time six months had passed.

Her dear husband was a schoolfellow of her father, she, Ninette, was an only child. She had passed examinations and worked for her living as means at home were small, her father being a painter of small renown.

Férin came to stay with his schoolfellow in Paris. After some time he had taken rooms in their neighbourhood, and her father and Férin had taken their walks together. " I," said Ninette, with a blush, " loved him the first day I saw him. Ah ! if you knew how good he is ! " One day her father had told her that Férin desired her for his wife, and that if his child was willing he had nothing to say against it. So Férin and Ninette were married, and lived close to the old painter. " You know, we never thought then that Mr. Férin would have to go out to Tonquin again." But of course there is always a cloud to the brightest of horizons. And this was the cloud :

When Férin had had a good look at his old parents, his brothers and sisters, their wives and husbands, the numerous nephews and nieces, had walked all the old walks and been happy for a month, and was beginning

to get tired of this long-wished-
for happiness, his mother said to
him one day, " Thou shouldest
marry, my son. Thou hast the
means and position. Hast thou
not taken a fancy to Caroline
or *la petite* Bernon ? "

No, Férin thought he had not.
But he smiled and said that he
was too old now, and would not
marry. His mother was a
cautious woman, so she let the
subject drop. Her son's assur-
ance that he intended to stay in
France if possible pacified the
old lady to some extent, and she
did not further press her son's
marriage for the time.

Then Férin went to Paris,
and he married Ninette. The
mother was taken by surprise,
and when, a month after the
wedding, Férin took his bride to
be introduced to his family, she
had but a cold greeting. For
years the old lady had said that
when her son came home she
would choose his wife for him.
And now, after all, he had chosen

for himself, *le vilain!* Ninette
was timid and warm-hearted, so
she felt this coldness very keenly.
But, after all, it must not signify;
Férin loved her and made her
happy. They went back to
Paris, and lived through two
happy years. It is at the end of
this time that Férin had to look
after this business in Tonquin,
and, after some consideration, it
was settled that Ninette should
go with her husband.

Now in our little bit of a place
everybody knows everybody else.
We all know also each other's
pedigree, past history, family
skeletons, and so on; if we do
not, we put in the details as best
we can. We have plenty of
leisure, and, when it is hot, bad
temper enough and to spare.
We make nasty remarks and say
disagreeable things because at
98° in the shade livers get
slightly enlarged, and one is not
amiable. But this is one thing
I have remarked, if there is some
real trouble or sorrow anywhere

there is a handful of people who
will do the right thing at the
right time.

We counted amongst our
numbers not a few scandal-
mongers, always ready for mischief, and with the general
inclination for idle talk was it
not a wonder that for almost
two years Ninette lived in peace
amongst us? Or was it, Ninette,
that you had made no enemies,
and through your gentle presence
hushed the busy gossips?

Time passed pleasantly. All
the winter we were very merry.
And then the spring came with
a wealth of flowers, the first hot
days and heavy showers.

We were to dine with the
Resident one evening. Ninette
was not there. A chit had come
in when we were sitting down,
saying that Mrs. Férin was in-
disposed and had to stay at
home. Her chair stood empty,
and somehow the dinner was
lengthy and quiet.

The next morning I had to go

to town ; as I passed Ninette's
house I went in to see how she
was. As nobody met me on the
way I went on to her room. I
stood a moment in the door ; a
great fear came over me. Why,
what had come over Ninette?
Was Ninette dying? Ninette
would never get well, I knew
that in an instant.

Ninette was in bed, white, thin,
changed, pain written in deep
lines on her face. The eyes were
double their usual size. She
lifted up her head as I entered,
and put her finger to her lips to
indicate that I was not to make
a noise.

"I am very ill, *mignonne*," she
said, in a weak, dry whisper.
"Dysentery," she said, and two
heavy tears ran down her poor
little whitened cheeks.

"Don't cry, *chérie*," I said.
"Come, I will stay with you and
make things comfortable. It is
nothing. I have had dysentery
myself. You must go home first
mail."

" Férin has just dropped off to
sleep. Oh, my poor boy ! *J'ai
peur.*"

There he was, poor man,
asleep on the verandah just outside her bedroom door, still in
his pyjamas. He had been up
all night, and the doctor had
been there too, and had just left
when I came in ; he was to send
a nurse from the hospital. It
seems that Ninette had been
ailing for some time, but had
attached no importance to her
indisposition. Yesterday morning things had suddenly taken a
bad turn. Quickly she had become worse, and by this morning
both husband and doctor had
become deeply alarmed. Still
where there is life there is hope.
Ninette was young, and would
pull through all right. I spoke
to her gently, fanning her the
while, for it was terribly hot. We
were now in July, and the heat
intense. Presently the nun from
the hospital came in, bright, cheer-
ful, and neat. I prepared to go.

" No, no, *chéric*, stay with me,"
pleaded Ninette.

And so that is how I stayed.

The slight noise of the good
sister's entry had wakened the
sleeper on the verandah; he
jumped up with a start painful
to behold, and ran to his wife's
bedside. What had been his
dreams, poor man ?

" *Ma mignonne tu vas mieux ?* "
he said, laying his cheek against
hers.

" Yes," she said, with a smile.

We left them and busied ourselves in the kitchen preparing
such food as might be needed
during the day. The good sister's face did not express much,
and I shrank from putting ques-
tions, so we went about our work
in silence. From time to time
the good sister knelt down in
silent prayer. And the day wore
on. Férin did not stir from his
wife's bedside. The heat all
that day was intense ; the servants predicted a typhoon. The
doctor came in every hour. He

had his hands full, as this heat
was filling the hospital. He
himself looked tired and care-
worn. Ninette's case affected
him deeply.

"Pooh," he said, after one of
his stays in the sick-room, wiping
the drops of perspiration from
his forehead, "after this I shall
be glad of my leave."

The evening came; the heat
was quite appalling. Not a
breath of air, not a sound.
Ninette was dying. She lay
motionless, her head deep back
in the cushions, her eyes half
closed, the lips dry and dis-
coloured. She took no more
notice of time and surroundings;
the pains were all gone, Ninette
suffered no more. Férin at her
side had her little hand in his.
Ah! poor man. He was calling
her by pet names, his very soul
was in his voice. At times
Ninette raised the heavy eyelids and looked at her husband.

It was eight o'clock now, and
quite dark. We had forced

Férin to take some food in the dining-room. The good sister had taken him, and was keeping him company. I was near Ninette, watching her lips and eyelids, in the hope that I might hear her sweet voice once more. Suddenly she sat up, her eyes wide open, looking straight over my shoulder.

"Who is there?" she gasped.

A dread horror seized me; I thought Ninette was raving. I looked round sharply. In the dim part of the room stood an Annamite woman. " *C'est moi. C'est Thiba.* "

" Thiba? It is true, then!" said Ninette, falling exhausted into her husband's arms, who had rushed back to her bedside at the first sound of her voice. He flung himself across her bed in hopeless despair.

" Ninette, my Ninette!" he pleaded, half crazy in his anguish.

But Ninette neither moved nor spoke. She lay quite still. A pale light lay on the young face, then lingered for awhile in her eyes, and Ninette had passed away.

Sleep well, sweet one!

When I looked up Thiba was gone, but where she had been standing I noticed a small bit of paper. I went to pick it up and as I unfolded it some greyish powder fell on the floor.

" It is a medicine paper," said the house-boy to whom I showed it, "and this is Annamite medicine."

Had Thiba heard of Ninette's illness, and had she come to try the healing powers of this powder? We never ascertained, for nobody ever saw Thiba again.

There was a sudden hot wind, a great noise in the trees. A puff of air blew out the candles. I made my way to the bed and put my hand on Férin's shoulder. "I am going home," I said.

No answer.

" There's a typhoon coming."

" Oh, go; leave me alone! Oh! my love, my love!"

" Poor friend ! "

I felt for Ninette's hand; it was cold. Yes, it was all over.

When I came out into the garden it was black night. I made out my boys' voices in the darkness, and somehow we got home; and only just in time. The storm burst over our town in pitiless fury. When the morning came half of our little colony was in ruins. Férin's home was wrecked. The coffin was put into the garden and stood under the shade of the magnolia-tree during the day. Friends sent what flowers the storm had left them, and oh! irony of all things mortal! a fresh, crisp breeze played amongst the ferns and palm-leaves and kept the funeral trappings in a gentle motion. At nightfall Ninette was carried to her resting-place. And so farewell, dear Tonquin friend !

THE RIVERSIDE PAGODA.

THE Tonquin river is the very life-blood of the country.

Tumultuously rapid in the uplands, its surging depths the homes of much-feared monsters, it rolls its yellow waves like great, broad ribbons through the fertile plains. Its beds are ever shifting, its banks are never stable. A sandy, gently descending, beach-like embankment here, the shore opposite rises steep and abruptly, undermined by the waves, the mere tread of a child's foot or the falling of a stone will send great slices of earth splashing into the water.

To-day there rolls the mighty stream, town and village to the

right and left, and green fields
nourished by its thousand water-
ways; and on its surface the
wood-built junks with big, swell-
ing fish-eyes painted at the bow,
their sails spread out like wings
of butterflies. And maybe in a
year, maybe overnight, the
stream is there no more, but in
its place a sandy desert, and
scarcely can the eye discern in
the misty distance the glimmer
of a silvery thread. Yonder flows
the river.

There is a pagoda by the riverside. It stands so close to the
water that at times the waves
splash against the stones of the
portico. Through a three-arched
entrance covered in by a two-
storied roof, across a small paved
courtyard, with here and there a
green or blue porcelain pot with
sikas and cactuses, we enter the
temple of the good spirit. It
is a small, brick-built building, its curling roof, porcelain
edged and ornamented at the
corners with red-tongued, shaly

pottery monsters, and beyond,
the quietude of the sacred wood.
There grows the banyan-tree,
shady and ever green, and,
clustering round, all sorts of
bushes. Here, unmolested, protected by the holy shades, meet
all the birds of the neighbourhood, breaking for awhile the
dead silence as they quit their
nests at dawn and come back
noisily at night. It is as
old as time itself, this little
place.

Years and years ago there was
no river here at all, but once
upon a time it rained in torrents
for fourteen days, and then it
stormed, and in the morning
there were the muddy waves of a
mighty stream where had been
paddy-fields before. On the
shore lay the white body of a
dead woman, and scattered about
fragments of a junk and relics of
a cargo. She was young and
beautiful. Her face yet bore
the traces of her struggle, and
her right hand was tightly closed

over a little silver bangle. It was a baby's arm ring.

The people from the villages spied the body in the morning and buried it, and to appease the spirit of the dead woman they built the pagoda by the riverside, and there it had been standing for many generations, restful and cool amidst the glorious landscape, and year by year the banyan-tree dropped new branches and its shade grew deeper and deeper.

At night sometimes a note of infinite sadness is borne on the wind, and in the villages around the mothers who are suckling little ones press closer to their breast each little head and say, " It is the good spirit by the riverside. She cannot sleep for she is sorrowing for her babe." And in the morning they go and take fresh offerings to her shrine to quiet her unrest.

And the fishermen sailing by say that when the water shall rise to the wall of the temple of the good spirit the river will disappear, and they bend three times in salutation, and fire crackers as they pass.

There is nothing more beautiful than the country around the pagoda by the riverside : so soft its tints of green, so luminous its air, so pink its mist at dawn, so clear its starlit night. The rice waves in the fields and the plain stretches its broad expanse unhindered to the horizon. There lies the little sleepy village all bathed in sunshine, well hidden by the bamboo hedge, its feathery tips sharply outlined against the bright blue of the sky.

The villagers work in the fields, the children mind the buffaloes.

In the village there stands a well-built house. It is the house of Hat, who is the rich man of the commune. Meah, the wife of Hat, sat in her chamber, her heart was full of sorrow. What did she care for her silk clothes, the golden beads, her precious bracelets, her home, the servants? She was a childless wife. A sickly woman married to an indulgent husband, she had gratified each passing fancy, yet was she not poorer than the poorest in her village?

Hat, her good husband, as gentle as a woman, loved her with a great love. He knew too well why Meah his wife sat silent in his house, and he grieved with her and was ageing before his time.

Meah could bear her grief no longer, and one day, bursting into tears, she begged her husband to take a second wife. Hat shook his head full of forebodings. "Was it not better to remain alone than bring a stranger to their home?" But Meah thought otherwise.

"I have already found a maid, if thou wilt let me do so," she insisted.

Now this is what had happened the night before. Some coolie women were carrying wood into the court and she was looking on. Amongst them there was a girl dressed in a few rags, thin, but withal looking strong and healthy. She had often noticed this girl before; her face was plain but pleasant, and she spoke in a gentle voice. A thought struck her like lightning: here was a wife for Hat.

When the women had finished carrying their wood she called the girl into her chamber, and a week later A-Thy was a member of Hat's household. A-Thy was the child of poor parents. Transplanted suddenly to this house of plenty, the half-starved girl bloomed quickly into womanhood. And Meah grew jealous. Never did the yellow-eyed monster find a more wretched victim. Due to her own persuasions, the presence of this other woman, younger, fairer than herself, whose very shadow filled her soul with tortures, yet must she keep her for her selfish ends. No peace by day, no rest at night. The

hideous worm gnawed till, ghastly
white, thin as a skeleton, she
haunted her own household, an
ever-present heartache to Hat,
her good husband.

Many times angry words were
rising to A-Thy's lips, but she
never spoke them, for she was
sorry in her heart for Meah, and
Hat was good to her. And they
had food at home. Since she
could remember starvation had
sat grimly in her home; she had
seen the old people wrapped in a
white cotton dress when dead,
and buried in a mat, too poor to
buy a coffin. But happy was
she when her son was born! A
great change came over Meah;
she lost her harsh manner towards A-Thy, and she, simple
soul, thought that the little one
would bring peace amongst them.

The baby was three months
old when one day Yongh came
from her village. She had never
cared much for the sulky fellow,
but now, so far from home, the
well-known face was an unex-

pected pleasure. A-Thy, so much alone, for she was neither maid nor mistress, listened eagerly to all the gossip from her little village.

Three days Yongh stayed with them, and it was on the evening of the third day that A-Thy was wanted in Meah's chamber. It was a rude awakening. Hat, flushed and angry, called her by a shameful name. Meah was as hard as a stone. They would give fifty piastres to Yongh if A-Thy would marry him. The child was theirs.

A-Thy lay weeping at Meah's feet, now crying, now raging, now explaining for the hundredth time that Yongh was nothing to her. But Meah had spoken : she wanted the baby all to herself.

What could A-Thy do?

When the evening came she, like a poor lost soul, was still roaming round the house. The door remained shut ; the dogs growled angrily behind the walls. At night she groped her way

10

across the fields to the pagoda
by the riverside; from time to
time she stopped and listened.
She fancied she could hear a
baby's cry; there, behind the
hedge, were the lights in Hat's
house. Within Meah had the
babe all to herself. It seemed
so sweet to hold it to her breast
at last in full possession. But
the baby cried, and, like an echo,
a note of infinite sadness came
borne up on the wind.

Through the banyan-tree the
first signs of dawn were peep-
ing faint and rose-hued. The
shadowy figures of a boy and
girl have just passed through
the portico; they cross the yard
and sit down under the porch of
the temple.

"A-Quaï," said the boy, "I
will look for water to bathe thy
weary feet."

"No, no; come and rest. Let
us stop here, and at daylight
we will on to Meah's house."
And, her head on Gang's

shoulder, she falls asleep as she speaks.

A low, sad moan of sorrow goes through the stillness of the night. The boy and girl press closer one against the other.

"What was that?" said A-Quaï, startled in her sleep. And there it was again.

"It is the good spirit of the temple," said Gang. And once more, long-drawn and sad.

"Gang," whispered A-Quaï, trembling with fear, "it is within. Listen!"

It was as if somebody was crying bitterly. Gang and A-Quaï hardly dared to breathe; too frightened to run away, they stayed till daylight, dispersing the shades of night, filled them with courage, and hand in hand they ventured to enter the sanctum.

It was still indeed within; the coarsely-hewn images looked peaceful enough. The sounds had died away, but there in the corner something was moving.

It was a young woman asleep
on the stones, her hair dis-
hevelled, her eyelids swollen with
crying. By her side lay a small
bundle, a stick, and a little tin
cup.

"Look," said A-Quaï, softly;
"she is a traveller like ourselves. But she has some great
sorrow."

The woman stirred uneasily
in her sleep.

"Shall we wake her and see if
we can do aught for her?"

But the woman was already
wakened by the sound of their
voices. She looked around bewildered, but, memory coming
back quickly at the sight of her
surroundings, her eyes filled
again with heavy tears.

"Sister, can we do naught for
thee?" inquired A-Quaï, greatly
moved by the sorrowful attitude
of the woman, who could be but
a few years older than herself.

"No, kind stranger, nobody
can help me."

"Come, sister, eat with us,"

begged Gang; "maybe we go the same road afterwards.

"I have food," said the woman, "but I don't want to eat."

Gang went to look for water, and A-Quaï induced the woman to follow her, and they sat down side by side under the porch. A-Quaï put a biscuit into the woman's hand. She carried it to her mouth, but, shaking her head, she said—

"I cannot eat; the food dries on my tongue. Thou dost not know, for thou hast had no children. My babe does want me. Oh! where shall A-Thy rest her weary head? Her eyes are blind."

"Then thy little one is dead?" asked A-Quaï.

"It is not dead; but it is mine no more."

Then, little by little, A-Thy told her story.

"Dost thou speak of Meah, the wife of Hat?"

"Yes," said the woman.

"She is my sister," said Gang

When the woman heard this she fell down before him on her knees and implored him with many tears to try and turn the heart of Meah, his sister.

"Cry no more," promised Gang; "we will help you."

The woman, trembling between fear and hope, took up her bundle and stick and fastened the cup to her waistband.

"Blessed be the good spirit who has sent you to poor A-Thy."

And so they parted—A-Thy to the left, Gang and A-Quaï to the right, to the village.

Here all was bustle, for the day was already well advanced. The women, as they drew water at the well, were talking about the good spirit by the riverside; how they had heard it in the night.

Meah was happy when she saw Gang enter with his wife. Brother and sister had not seen each other since the feast of the *Têt*. Meah, with the babe in her

arms, was a new woman. Fresh
life within her frail body, she
went about her house ordering a
meal of welcome and preparing
a chamber for A-Quaï; and Hat,
like a man who has awakened
from a nightmare sleep, sat with
a broad smile on his good face.

But the babe fretted. He
would not take his food. Already round his little mouth two
wrinkles grew like lines of sorrow.

"'Thou must send for a nurse,
Meah," said A-Quaï, when she
saw the little face.

And Meah sent a messenger
to the villages around for a
nurse; and A-Thy's babe was
suckled by a hired woman.

An evil spirit had breathed
across the village. At night,
when all was still, a note of
infinite sadness came borne up
on the wind. The mothers sat
up and listened, and there it was
again. In the morning they went
and carried offerings to the shrine
of the good spirit.

At night two babes had sick-

ened, three more the day after,
and by the end of the week there
was a great silence in the village.
No little bare feet pattering in
the sand, no games around the
wooden pillars of the stranger's
house. Within the huts there
lay the little sufferers, big-eyed
and feverish, like plants that
had been blighted overnight.

One died, and then another,
and still another, and the dole-
ful lamentations of the wailing
women could be heard from
morn till night, and all through
the dark they rose in mournful
monotony.

Then did the shaven old village bonze, brown-clothed and
toothless, sit in deep reflection,
and the outcome of his sombre
musings was that he ordered a
special procession to be organised
before sundown, so as to be
pleasing in the eyes of the good
spirit by the riverside, who was
evidently in deep wrath.

To the sound of gongs and the
beating of tam-tams the whole

village filed out in long procession, and repaired to the pagoda by the riverside, breaking noisily upon its peaceful silence. And the old bonze saluted the shrines and bowed to the ground. A feast was served in the court, of which all the villagers partook, and as they ate of the good things set before them hope revived, and when the shadows deepened round the banyan-tree they returned to their village with brightened faces.

But who can reason with the dead? Especially when the dead one is the ghost of a woman? There is no faith in women, saith the wise man.

It is certain that the good spirit by the riverside, unheeding the offerings of peace, continued in her wrath.

The babes died as before. Soon each house had its coffin. The traveller who passed by at night might hear the wailing through the bamboo hedge, and from the pagoda by the riverside came back that same feared note of sadness.

Meah was ever hovering round A-Thy's babe. Care sat on her brow, for, in spite of the nurse, it was not thriving ; still, of all the children in the village it was the only one that had escaped the fever.

A-Quaï, too, was quiet and thoughtful ; she had never breathed a word of their encounter with A-Thy in the pagoda.

Alone at night, for Gang, her husband, had gone to find the body of her old grandmother and give her burial in her native village, she thought many things. She listened to the weary tread of Meah's slippered feet backwards and forwards, carrying the baby in her arms and singing softly. And then there arose the wretched wailing from the hired mourners, and, long-drawn and clear, the fearful echo from the river.

Long was the sleepless watch.

Slowly the whole truth dawned
on A-Quaï. It was A-Thy's babe
that was doing the mischief.

She would go to the sorcerer
and get his advice, lest the whole
village perish through the anger
of the good spirit. Next evening,
under the cover of night, a
handkerchief drawn well over
her head, she went to a much-
renowned sorcerer in a neighbouring village. In a few words
she told him her story, and the
wise man, who had already
heard of the calamity that had
befallen his neighbours, promised
a visit for the following day.

The sorcerer came, and it was
just· as A-Quaï had thought :
A-Thy's babe was doing the
mischief.

" A-Thy's baby to be taken to
the temple of the good spirit, for
its presence in Meah's house
was displeasing to the *mâne*."

The holy man had spoken.

It spread through the village
like fire. The crying ceased.
All, men and women, hurried to

the stranger's house, where they found the old bonze already ranging his gongs and tam-tams. And then away all in procession to Meah's house.

But Meah had shut her doors, and, pale as death, refused resolutely to comply with the orders of the holy men.

Deafening was the noise of the tam-tams and the gongs and the clamouring of many voices. But Meah sat in sullen silence in her chamber. A-Quaï, who was near her, held her peace.

"It seems to me that the babe does sleep a heavy sleep in all this noise," said Meah, and parted the curtains over her couch to look at the child.

Her face grew ghastly white. She picked it up hastily and brought it to the light.

"It is dead," said A-Quaï.

Meah laughed, her lips drawn with pain. "They may have it now," she said. Her legs failed her, and she fell back on the couch.

"Thou wilt bring naught but sorrow to the house of Hat. Scht! be silent. If they should hear outside the child is dead, it will fare badly with thee and thine. Give me a cloth," and quickly she wrapped the child in some garment and went before the door.

As A-Quaï, with the child in her arms, stepped amongst them she was greeted by shouts of joy, and with renewed vigour they beat their tam-tams and their gongs, and all formed quickly into procession, and away to the pagoda by the river. A-Quaï walked between the bonze and the sorcerer.

Frightful was the beating, the holy men bent till their foreheads touched the very dust, and, lifting the child three times above their heads, they laid it at the foot of a stone image. Then the people hurried back to the village.

It is already dark, and the

moon has risen behind the banyan-tree.

A woman has just passed into the court. The moonlight falls full upon her face. Is it thee, A - Thy? Thin, half - naked, famished, she sinks down near the image, close to the little bundle at its feet.

She saw it and undid the cloth. "It is my babe," she murmured, "but it is dead."

"Cry not, A-Thy," said a gentle voice, "for the baby is not dead. Open its lips and pour in some of this liquid, and then go to the river and bathe its face and rub its body with the cloth. Peace be with thee and thy babe, A-Thy."

And in the morning, when the people from the village came to the temple, the child was gone, and they rejoiced, for they said the good spirit had come to fetch it, and they went back and feasted.

But Meah, the wife of Hat, sat at home and wept.

HAND-FED.

MR. and Mrs. Philipin lived in the little white house at the end of the road. Mr. Philipin had been a small Government functionary in Cochin China, and when he left the service and got his pension he and his wife came to Tonquin to settle. They bought a small plot of ground, had it reclaimed, built a house and planted a garden.

Everybody in the town knew Mr. and Mrs. Philipin. There were one or two peculiarities about them. They were both small and resembled each other, they had round, kindly faces, and had preserved a rosy complexion.

They had no children but always
addressed each other as "papa"
and "maman," and it was only
on occasions of exceptional importance that Mr. Philipin called
his wife "Rosine" and maman
retorted with "Jean Philipin."
Mrs. Philipin had, moreover, a
conservative tendency in her
toilette. Her dresses were all
made after the fashion of those
worn when she first came out,
and that was many years ago.

Though everybody knew them,
they never showed at any of the
gatherings of the town. They
lived one for the other and both
for their garden.

Their little white house amidst
the flourishing shrubs was the
cosiest of nests! Three square
rooms, the centre one the dining-
room, to the left a bedroom,
to the right a sitting-room. A
verandah was built out in front
and made shady by green blinds,
flower-pots stood on the steps
leading into the garden. And
within and without everything

was beautifully clean and neat. Mrs. Rosine looked to everything herself, for she despised colonist ways.

Jean Philipin, in shirt-sleeves, was working in the back garden.

Maman is smoothing her hair before the looking-glass in the bedroom and putting on her sun hat. Then she picks up her umbrella and draws on a pair of mittens.

"Well, Jean Philipin, I am going," she calls out into the garden.

"*Bien, bien*, Rosine. My compliments to the good Sister Maria. I shall see to everything."

He has left his spade, and, after having wiped his face on his sleeve, he gives her two hearty kisses on each cheek. A minute later Mrs. Rosine disappears through the little gate in the front garden and walks down the road. Jean Philipin stands in the road and looks after her. When she reaches the corner

she turns round and kisses her
hand to him.

Whenever one or the other
went to town, that is to say
walked up their road and the
one that crossed it and into the
principal street running parallel
with the river to the three or
four stores congregating round
the bank building, there was
always this tender leave taking.
Once, though, Rosine had turned
the corner without throwing back
her kiss.

When she returned from her
outing she could see at once that
something was wrong. For when
Mrs. Rosine greeted her husband
and told him that she had brought
a piece of fresh cheese just out of
the mail ice-box, Jean Philipin
got very red in the face and said
"he thought these mail cheeses
were not nearly as nice as they
might be." Those were his very
words.

Of course he could not keep it
up any length of time. After he
had said that Rosine ought to

wear coloured stockings like the other ladies, and that he thought the cook made onion soup very well, Rosine, utterly bewildered and crushed, sat down and cried.

Then all came to light. Rosine had taken no heed of her husband as he stood in the middle of the road, and had turned the corner as unconcernedly as any young girl.

And Rosine explained: if Jean Philipin had not at once turned into the house in a tiff he would have noticed a gentleman coming up the road close behind him. Now if Rosine had kissed her hand might not this gentleman have taken it for himself?

So all was settled and peace was made, but the bend of the road is called to this day the kissing corner.

Madame Rosine walked on past the Residence till she came to the hospital. Here she asked for Sister Maria.

" Well, madame," said the good sister, after they had exchanged greetings and were sitting in Sister Maria's cool whitewashed parlour, " I think I have got what you want. Just wait a minute." And she went outside and came back with a bundle in her arms. " Now what do you think of that ? " inquired Sister Maria, as she was undoing the bundle and holding up for inspection an Annamite baby which might be four or five days old. " You know they are never very beautiful at first. Do you remember Madame Durand's first baby ? it certainly was very plain, and now I call it a very pretty child. It is a little girl, and we have christened her and called her Fleurette."

" Dear me, it is a very pretty name. Poor little thing. Let me hold her a minute." And while she was doing so Sister Maria told her how they found a small bundle on the verandah early in the morning, and that when they had opened it they saw it contained this baby. The

sisters behaved very foolishly;
they wanted to keep it, and they
ran at once for warm water to
give it a bath and milk to feed it.
She was sorry they could not
keep the little foundling, but as
yet they had nowhere to put it.
So she had written at once to
Mrs. Philipin to tell her what
had happened.

For a long time the Philipins
had wanted to adopt an Annamite child, a girl by preference.
Their property was all in the
country, here it produced just
enough to give them a comfortable living, transferred elsewhere
it would not suffice. It was
therefore likely that they would
spend their last years where they
were. Besides, after so many
years of life in the East, they
feared the cold of the North.
They had no near relations
living, and they thought it would
be a comfort to have a child
around them now they were
growing older. So, after a little
more conversation with Sister

Maria, Mrs. Rosine wrapped the child up again and returned home.

Jean Philipin was sitting under the verandah enjoying the evening breeze. He jumped up when he heard the turning of the front gate and saw his wife cross the garden.

That was a memorable evening in the little house at the end of the road.

Jean Philipin had been put into a long chair, and, armed with an improved feeding bottle, had been told to give the babe its supper, while maman went inside to make a temporary cradle out of a basket covered with a mosquito curtain.

It was the apothecary who let out the secret. He declared upon his honour there was a baby at the Philipins, he had just sold an improved feeding bottle and a box of tinned milk to Monsieur Jean Philipin.

The apothecary was always dosing them with something or

other. Some shrugged their
shoulders and went home, but
one or two of the more curious
went down the road in the evening after dinner, and looking
into the lighted dining-room they
saw Jean Philipin carrying a
sleeping baby backwards and
forwards.

He, who was wit and scandal-
monger in one, when he saw this,
burst into uncontrollable fits of
laughter, and, unable to go to
sleep without mastering the
brown - hued mystery in Jean
Philipin's arms, went straight
into the dining-room and inquired
what the meaning of all this
was.

The wit went home, and when
he turned into the road, to which
the one lonely palm gives its
name, and where the neighbours
walk about on summer evenings
discussing the events of the day,
he was able to confirm the state-
ment of the apothecary and give a
detailed description of Fleurette's
charms.

Not a soul could understand the matter. Whatever were the Philipins thinking about ? At their time of life, and of all things this wretched little native waif and stray! There was a good deal of croaking. But neverthe- less the Philipins kept their baby, and were as happy and proud over it as possible.

They had their fixed plans about the little girl. They would always speak French to her, and forbid the servants to address her in their tongue, so as to re- move her as much as possible from native influence. She should be taught how to look after the house, the cooking, the linen, and learn her catechism when she would be twelve years old. She should wear European clothes, and if they could find a suitable husband for her when she had reached a marriageable age she should be married, and they would give her a small *dot*, and the young couple should live near them.

In the following years nothing happened to interfere with the fulfilment of their plans. Fleurette spoke French very well, and mastered the secrets of Mrs. Rosine's good housewifery. And all this time she was a well-known little figure in the town. On Sunday evenings, one hand in each of the old people's, they went for a walk. The Annamites took off their hats as they passed, and stood open-mouthed from sheer admiration.

Who does not remember Fleurette? Her odd old-fashioned clothes, the broad-brimmed hat trimmed with a pink ribbon and tied under the chin, her little white frock, much starched and embellished with numerous tucks, her drawers frilled round the bottom and hanging down to the middle of her leg, the little white socks and black shoes? Her black hair was tied into a plait at the back of her head, and in the snowy whiteness how brown seemed the skin!

Then came the time of the
catechism and Fleurette partook
of her first communion, and took
possession of a small bedroom
built on to the room of the old
people.

Then more years passed by in
uneventful placitude. And so,
little by little, Fleurette grew
into a tall, shapely girl. If, instead of her unbecoming, old-
fashioned home-made frocks, she
had worn her own native garb
she would have been a pretty
Annamite girl.

But even as she was she had
her admirers. There was one
young fellow, an interpreter at
the court, who thought that if
he could but find favour in
Fleurette's eyes he would be the
happiest of men. Jean Philipin
and his wife looked favourably
on the interpreter. He was a
Saigonese, well instructed, and a
Catholic like Fleurette, and quite
able to support a wife. When
he therefore asked for the girl's
hand, there was nothing to

their mind to prevent a happy union.

But Fleurette in the meantime was doing a foolish thing. She was giving her heart away to Atack. Atack was the house-boy. He had been in the Philipins' service for more than a year, he was a good-looking, though worthless, fellow, and the girl's love for the boy, though a secret to her good guardians, had long been confessed to Atack. Many times the girl had been on the verge of telling "maman" everything, but the moment she opened her mouth the words died on her lips. How could she tell them that she, Fleurette, who had been reared like their child, who had lived for all these years surrounded by their cares, how could she tell them that she loved Atack the house-boy?

What miserable moments she had passed when, left to her sewing, the old people dozing in their chairs through the hot afternoon, she had put down her work to think. And while she was still thinking she heard the voice of Atack calling her in the garden, and where then were her good resolutions ? They came to nothing, and when one even· ing, after a somewhat prolonged visit of the interpreter, maman came into Fleurette's room, she found it empty. She went into the garden and called her by her name, but the girl was nowhere to be found. She returned into Fleurette's room, and it struck her that its general aspect was changed. On the bed lay the dress Fleurette had been wearing during that day, on the chair close by lay her linen, and under it her shoes. A little statue of the Holy Virgin which used to hang above her bed had been removed.

She went into the front garden, where her husband was smoking his pipe and watering his pet flowers.

"Jean Philipin," she called, "have you seen Fleurette any- where ? "

"No, my friend, I have not seen her since dinner," and he went on watering his flowers.

Rosine, deeply concerned, went again into Fleurette's room and then into the kitchen, where she questioned the cook. No, he had not seen or heard anything, but, "if madame would not be angry," the house-boy had gone away, for his grandfather had died, and he had left at once; as he did not like to disturb madame he had said nothing.

"Jean Philipin," said Rosine, as she came back once more into the back garden, "I cannot find Fleurette anywhere. Come and see."

They went together into the back garden and called her. Then they went into her bed-room, and Rosine pointed to the dress on the bed and the empty spot where the statue had been hanging. The good old people had been growing very serious, and their faces betrayed their anxiety, but they did not like

to put their thoughts into
words.

"Go and sit down in the
verandah, my darling, while I
go and speak to the cook."

Rosine sat down while her
husband went into the kitchen.
She could not rest, and she
walked to and fro looking up
and down the road that passed
their house. It was so dark
already, and Fleurette had never
walked a step without her, not
even to go to see the good sisters
at the hospital. What could have
happened to the child?

While she was thus puzzling
her brains in unprofitable specu-
lation loud shrieks rose from the
cook-room, and when she came
there she found her husband
beating the cook with a stick.

"And now go away this in-
stant, you scoundrel, you liar!"
she heard Jean Philipin say, as
he was shutting the garden door
behind the cook's quickly retreat-
ing figure. A minute later he
had disappeared down the darken-

ing road. Jean Philipin mopped
his head ; he was very white
round the lips, and his hands
were trembling.

"Rosine," he said, and he
took his wife's hand caressingly
into his, "Fleurette has left us
of her own free will. She has
gone with Atack. It is a shame.
But if the girl could do that to
us, the less we talk about it the
better."

Rosine could not speak, and
the tears fell one by one on Jean
Philipin's hand.

They sat a long time in silence
under the verandah—Jean Philipin full of angry thoughts, but his
wife tortured by remorse. How
could she have been so blind as
not to have seen what was going
on in the girl's mind ?

At last Mr. Philipin went to
lock the front door, and they
went to bed. He tossed about
uneasily for some time and went
to sleep. Not so his wife. As
soon as she noticed the peaceful
breathing of her husband, she

slipped away, unlocked the front door, and put a light into Fleurette's room.

She did not know herself what she was hoping, but she could not believe that the child could leave them like that.

The next morning the candle in Fleurette's room had burnt out and hundreds of insects lay scorched around it. The girl had not come back.

When they saw that the child had indeed left them they abolished "papa" and "maman," and became plain Jean Philipin and Rosine for all occasions, and consigned the memory of Fleurette to oblivion.

Rosine had a secret. The morning after the departure of the good-for-nothings, as she was arranging the things in the dining-room, she discovered that two of her silver table-spoons were missing.

"So the girl had gone with a thief," thought Rosine, crying with painful emotion; and she

wished she had never brought
the little girl into their house.

Many miles away from Fleurette's old happy home there
stood a hut. It was built of
mud and covered over with palm
leaves. It stood quite alone in
the middle of a limestone quarry
which used to be worked by
Chinamen. Now, but for this
one lonely habitation, it is
deserted.

The hut could not be seen
from the river, for it was well
hidden by the rocks; it over-
looked to the north an admir-
able bit of country. Waving
fields, neatly divided by narrow,
somewhat elevated footpaths;
here and there a watchman's
diminutive hut, raised on bamboo scaffolding, stood isolated in
the fields; and in the distance
palms and banana-trees over-
topping the bamboo hedge of
some village.

The quarry was held in bad
repute by the villagers. When
the Chinamen used to work

12

there they took the girls of
the village and shipped them
to China. Since they had left
a tiger had been seen from time
to time, and it was believed that
he slept in one of the caverns of
the quarry.

An old man called Bat lived
all by himself in the hut amongst
the limestone. Sometimes he
could be seen—a little withered
old man with scanty grey hair
on his head and two or three
bushy tufts on his upper lip—
cutting stones in the sunshine.
He had a *sampan* on the river,
and when he had cut a few
stones he would load his boat,
fasten the door of his hut, and
sail away down the river. He
might stay away a week or a
fortnight or more, nobody noticed his absence. When he
came back he moored his boat
to the shore, climbed the rocks,
and disappeared within the hut.
And there he would remain
sometimes three or four days
together. Then, one fine morn-

ing, he would unlock his door,
looking thinner and older than
ever, and go and cut stones in
the sunshine and take them
away down the river as before.

The people in the villages
were afraid of old Bat. They
believed him to be something of
a sorcerer. For a long time the
hut in the quarry had stood
empty, and one day some children who had strayed up the hill
were frightened by the sudden
appearance of a very old man.
They ran screaming down the hill.

"The tiger! the tiger!" they
cried.

Since then the old man in
the quarry had grown a more
familiar, if not a popular figure.

Old Bat was not a sorcerer,
but he was more—he was an
opium-smoker. He would work
till he had enough for a cargo
for his boat, and sail down the
river and sell the stones to a
builder. The money went to
purchase the drug. He gave
no thought to food; he would

eat anything, and the smallest
bit was sufficient.

From time to time, when he
had been to town, he would not
quit his hut for many days, and
when he did his face was terrible
to behold.

It was on a lovely morning
in the beginning of April that
an Annamite and a very young-
looking girl were climbing up the
rocks at the quarry. The hut
stood open, and they could see
the old man sitting in the sun
cutting his stones.

Atack called out to him, and
the old man turned round.

" He is a very old man, thy
grandfather," whispered Fleurette, frightened at the little
withered face.

" Yes," answered Atack, " he
is very old."

The old man was hard of
hearing and slow of speech, he
did but half understand what
his grandson was telling him.

" Hast thou brought any
money ? " he inquired.

"Go within and rest," said
Atack to Fleurette, "while I
talk to the old man."

Fleurette entered the hut but
came out again immediately.
The sickly fumes of opium lay
heavy in the small room. She
sat down outside and looked
into the landscape unfolding its
glorious panorama at her feet.

Fleurette's little face was very
sad, there was no trace there of
the joy that was throbbing everywhere that morning.

Slowly, in spite of her strug-
gling against it, the conviction
was gaining upon her that she
had done an awful thing.

Not love Atack! That was
impossible, as that love had
come to her unbidden. No. But
how was she fitted to be an
Annamite's wife?

Now she wore native clothes;
for three days she had lived and
fed like her husband. Food and
clothes were nothing—she would
learn to relish the one and adapt
herself to the other. But there

were things more subtle than
these—there was the teaching
of Jean Philipin and Rosine ;
and, though she had not lost
her dark skin, she was yet no
Annamite.

But Fleurette felt that even
this was nothing if she could
have loved Atack to-day as she
loved him when she had left her
home to follow him.

Unaccustomed as she was to
walking, her slippers hurt her
much, and their continued beating on her heels had made them
very sore.　While Atack had
gone into a village to get some
food, and she was resting under
a tree, she undid their bundle to
get something to wrap round her
aching heels.　As she was doing
so two silver tablespoons fell
with a ring to the ground.

Fleurette sat and looked at
them, too bewildered for a clear
thought.

When she saw Atack in the
road, she picked them up and
ran to meet him.

"I found these in the bundle.
How did they get into it?"

Atack had paled a little at the
sight of the spoons, and an embarrassed smile was quivering
round his lips.

"Well," he retorted, with
some show of defiance, "I took
them."

"Then they must be taken
back, Atack."

Atack lost his temper. They
argued hopelessly all through
the day, and Fleurette saw that
one did not understand the other.

In the evening they came to
a pagoda, and Fleurette took her
husband's hand and said—

"Thou knowest, Atack, that I
love thee better than myself. I
will in all things be obedient to
thee. Give me those spoons as
a present."

This request seemed to Atack
even more absurd than the pro-
posal to carry them back to his
old mistress, but he loved the girl
in his way, and so he promised
that the spoons should be hers.

The sickly fumes reached her even where she was sitting in front of the hut.

The girl, whose soul was already so full of sadness, was crying with weariness and disgust. So this was Atack's grandfather, an opium-smoker. Her girlish imagination had fancied him as a kindly old man, like one of those old ones she loved as a child, who used to pass their house, and when they saw the little girl would say a few words of greeting. The old folks of her country are so good to little ones. But he was not like one of them, a hideous skeleton, trembling in every limb, and she was afraid of him.

When Atack joined her in front of the hut she dried her tears and greeted him with a smile. He had had a long conversation with the old man. They would build a new hut for themselves, and the old man would keep the old one. For some time they would have to manage as best they could ; the old man would sleep in a cavern. Atack would cut stones too ; it would give them enough to provide their food and clothes.

The rest of the day passed quickly, for they were all three busy. The old man worked at the stones, and Fleurette and Atack cleaned the hut and made it habitable for the night.

As they sat all three round the rice-pot at their evening meal, and the country looked so peaceful and beautiful, new hope came to Fleurette, and when she went to rest soon after, she fell asleep at once.

Whether it was some sudden noise or a dream Fleurette could not tell, she awoke suddenly in the middle of the night and found herself sitting up on her couch listening, and yet she could hear nothing. She saw that she was alone, and that the door was open. It was a moonlit night, and outside the silvery light lay everywhere.

Fleurette called for Atack, but nobody answered. A vague terror seized her, and she slipped from her couch and passed through the door into the moonshine. The limestone looked white, and sparkled as if studded with many gems. Fleurette called again. Not a sound disturbed the stillness of the radiant night. She stood there for a long time, calling out from time to time. At last she noticed a faint light in one of the caverns; she followed the glimmer through the wilderness of stones, and reached a small hollow overhung by rocks, forming a well-sheltered retreat. On the floor was spread out a mat, and on it lay the old man and Atack, both asleep. Between them burnt the opium lamp, and the pipe itself had fallen to the ground. The sickly fumes of the drug hung round the rocks in bluish vapours.

Fleurette looked at the unconscious men in horror and disgust.

Fleurette crept back to her couch. The future rose before her in all its uncompromising ugliness; she knew now that whatever she might do she would have to suffer.

And she did suffer untold miseries.

After a very short time Atack did not try to hide his vice. The two men worked only to procure the drug. For days Fleurette was alone in the hut, half-naked and without food.

When the men came back after one of their expeditions Atack gave her some provisions, and the two men retired to their couches and smoked, oblivious of the rest of the world.

But what tortured Fleurette night and day was the knowledge that they had firearms. Where did they get them from, and for what purpose? From time to time she saw a rifle,

sometimes two, then again a
revolver or a parcel of ammunition. Many times Fleurette
thought she would run away
or kill herself, but always a
vague presentiment of some
frightful fate overtaking her
husband if she left him retained
her. She stayed in her wretched
home amongst the rocks to the
bitter end. And the end was
not far off.

It had been very hot that day,
and both Jean Philipin and his
wife Rosine were retiring to rest
rather later than usual.

They could not sleep. Hardly
had they drawn the mosquito
curtain when Mrs. Philipin declared that her husband had not
locked the front door. When it
had been proved that the door
was all right, Jean Philipin
fancied he heard footsteps in the
garden. But it was nothing.
They could not get rid of a
vague feeling of uneasiness, and
finally, to please his wife, Jean
Philipin got up and looked to

his revolver, which was hanging
at his side of the bed. It was
loaded and all right, and at last
they went to sleep.

But they had not been sleeping more than a quarter of an
hour when one of the shutters
was gently pushed open from
the outside, and a miserably-
dressed woman, thin and hag-
gard, passed noiselessly into the
room.

She looked at the sleepers.
Then she crouched down, and,
keeping in the shade thrown by
the furniture, crept to the wall
where the revolver was hanging.
With infinite care and precaution
she unfastened it, and then she
hid between the folds of a curtain and a wardrobe.

The old people slept peacefully.

A second time the shutters
were opened from the outside.
It was a man who came in, cat-
like and soft-footed ; he had a
revolver in his hand, a knife
between his teeth.

The moment he entered the room the woman sprang from her hiding-place, and putting herself between the bed and the man, she raised her weapon slowly without saying a word.

When the man had seen the woman he had sprung back in surprise, then his face grew convulsed with rage; he halted a moment while his breath came fast, then he took deliberate aim, and two shots were fired simultaneously. The woman fell on her face, the man disappeared into the darkness.

When the old people had sufficiently recovered from their fright to look around, they saw that one of the shutters leading into the garden stood open and on the floor near it lay the body of a woman bleeding heavily from a wound in her side. In her right hand she grasped Jean Philipin's revolver.

The noise of the shots had roused the cook in the outhouse. He was at once despatched to fetch Dr. Borne from the hospital, and to call out for the police at the corner of the road. As their house stood very isolated they had to wait some time before they could get any help.

Mrs. Rosine, overcoming her feelings, bravely helped her husband to raise the bleeding woman on to their bed.

Rosine bent over the white face with a startled cry.

" It is Fleurette," she gasped.

Fleurette heard her name, and she came back to life just for a while. Her eyes looked tenderly at the two old faces bending over her. Her eyelids trembled and her lips moved.

Rosine put her ear close to Fleurette's mouth. She caught these words : " Parcel inside my dress for you. Kiss Fleurette, maman."

And Fleurette's eyes clouded over, and she was dead.

Dr. Borne came just ¡as Fleurette had breathed her last.

The policemen were busy
following up a trail of blood
running right through the garden
and down the road. That little
crimson trail is your doom,
Atack !

Eight days later he and the
old man had their heads cut
off for smuggling firearms and
piracy. Early in the morning,
when the first sign of dawn came
across the grey fields, they died
without a word, their brains deep
in the realms of poppyland.

Inside Fleurette's miserable
gown, quite close to that terrible
wound, was found a parcel. It
contained two silver tablespoons.

IN THE VILLAGE.

OME years ago Doson was a small fishing village known intimately to but a few of the Europeans. On the beach there stood a low, whitewashed building of generous dimensions, thatched with straw. This was the Doson Hotel. In the winter shut up, it was left a prey to the storms, and the sand lay piled up in great heaps against the wall facing windward. In the summer parties of two and three would come to dream away a lazy day on the beach, with a bath at sundown. Others, more enterprising, with a rifle, plenty of ammunition, and copious provisions, would go inland, to come back presently, hot and footsore, to shoot at empty soda-water bottles under the shade of the verandah.

It was sundown on a day of December. The light had already faded out of the sky, the softly undulating country lay steeped in shades of violet. There in the distance stood the whitewashed hostelry, a small, shimmering speck on the grey brown sands, and the sea and the heavens streaked all over with yellow, and the beach full of life.

The fishermen are pulling in their nets. Wiry, naked, dark-hued fellows, small of stature, and older men, whose skin looks as if the sun had griddled it. Playing in the sand, or sitting about in groups, is a crowd of children and old folks; boys and girls of all sizes, old men and women in every stage of dilapidation. They all carry some sort of basket.

The fishermen pull away to a

rhythmic note of mutual encou-
ragement, bursting forth at each
haul at the nets. The nets
brought ashore, the fish are
turned out on the beach. There
they lie, dripping and open-
mouthed. Fish, crabs, shrimps
of all kinds, many-coloured and
of all sizes; great gasping monsters and pretty small fry. They
are soon sorted and piled into
baskets and on flat bamboo-
plaited trays. The work done,
the crowd comes in for the
leavings: the smallest of the
small fish, the baby crabs, hundreds of nameless fishy odds and
ends. All and everything is
picked up, till the tiniest bit has
found its appropriator.

One girl looks on, her basket
empty. Crouched comfortably
in the soft sand, she has her
chin between her hands and
blinks dreamily at the sea.
Then one by one the old folks
and the young make for their
villages inland. Many of them
have to walk far, and the night

is dark before they see the light
of their homesteads. A handful
of children, an old man who
walks with a stick, and a black,
scraggy dog, make their way
across the paddy-fields. They
walk in single file on the narrow
path; ahead a girl, straight, slim,
and brown as a berry, the scraggy
dog at her side. It is the same
girl who sat on the beach looking
at the sea.

Banh is telling stories. Her
young voice rings out clear and
distinct in the great stillness of
the evening. It is a wonderful
tale, all about a speechless
princess, a red-mouthed dragon,
and how the blue-winged adder,
who was a witch, came and
stung the princess, and how the
noble lady sickened ; and then
how the one who was like the
full moon killed the adder and
the dragon, and made the princess, whose tongue had been
loosened by her great fear, queen
in his kingdom.

" Goose-tail," said the girl,

just as the princess had been properly installed to the listeners' entire satisfaction, and laying her hand on the arm of a boy of her own size, who was dropping a shrimp into her basket previous to taking the side-path to his village—" Goose-tail, two from thee."

" Yes, two," said the other children.

" Why ? " said the boy, embarrassed by this sudden outbreak.

" Didst thou think, Goose-tail, I did not see thee last night crawl away to thy own sty, like a dirty one ? Thou didst forget about the fish ? Thou shalt never again, though. Two, I say. No, none of thy one-legged crabs. Big ones. There, that will do," and, with a good kick well applied to the small of his back, she sent the boy and his basket into the wet of the paddy-field. " And mark that, ye others," she said, facing the other children, her brown face

a shade darker through the angry
red, her small snub nose, a
little flattened at the nostrils,
well in the air, and her black
eyes all ablaze. " Mark ye that,
children. If ye think a fish be
too much, ye can speak. Ye
need not walk my road. Pooh!
ye are all miserable beggars ! "

There rose a clamour of pro-
testations all round. Had not
Banh always told them stories,
and had they not always paid
their fish ? No, rather would
they give her two than that they
should miss the story-teller who
made the little bare feet forget
the weary road. Banh, somewhat calmed, walked on, till, with
four other children, the old man,
and the black dog, she reached
their own village.

As they passed a brick-built
house, the only one in the village
besides the little pagoda of the
good spirit, Banh turned round
and said to the old man—

" When Beo-ben gives thee
thy rice, tell her Banh will

come to-morrow morning and sew."

"It is well, my daughter," and with a greeting the old man disappears within.

Somewhat away from the others there stands a small hut of the poorest kind; it is Banh's home. The door is still open. Opposite to the door the red *tablettes* with the names of the dead ancestors, to the left a bamboo framework covered with matting hung round with some brownish stuff mosquito curtains; in one corner a small cupboard, with a Chinese lock, a terra-cotta jar, holding drinking water, a bag of rice, a pewter joss-stick holder, some pots and pans. Leaning against the wall to the right a table, and on it lollipops, a few biscuits marked with red letters, on bamboo sprigs some things that look like green olives, a few oranges and bananas. All day long old Nguyen sits in front of her hut with this table; it is the village sweet shop. Now she is busy filling rice out of an earthenware pot into two cups, and ranging them round a saucer of soy standing on a mat on the floor.

"There," said Banh, putting her basket of fish in front of the old woman, who is trying to rekindle the fire under a pot of water. The old woman looked critically at the provisions.

"Lazy girl!" she scolded, as she put the bits one by one into the pot, "I have not seen thee all day long. My old bones are broken. What help dost thou give me in my old age? I would go to fetch the fish myself but that I fear thou wouldst give away my goods, and old Nguyen might go a-begging in the village."

Banh, unconcerned and light-hearted, did not listen. She picked up the husk of a cocoa-nut, dipped some water out of the jar, went in front of the door, sprinkled it over her feet, and, rubbing one against the other, freed them from the dust of the road.

"I should have sold thee to the Chinese long ago, then I would have had money for my old days. Oh, yes, a fine one thou wouldst have made," said Nguyen, in despair, putting her hands over her ears as Banh burst into the high falsetto of a Chinese love ditty.

The black dog pushed up to the wall and howled dismally.

Breaking off in the middle of a whimsical shriek, Banh sat down near the old woman on the mat, and, flattening her nose against Nguyen's cheek, she said—

"Grandmother, be kind to thy daughter's child; to-morrow I will bring thee lots of fish."

Nguyen shook her head, and they ate their rice and the fish in silence. The meal finished, the old woman pushed the cooking utensils in a corner, brought forth a parcel of red paper and some glue, trimmed the small oil lamp, and set to work to

make fire-crackers. Her slender fingers were restlessly busy,
a thousand little red paper tubes
for a few sapeques !

Banh, sitting on the bed, her
bare legs crossed tailor fashion,
had unfastened her blue handkerchief, and with a wide-toothed
wooden comb was smoothing her
glossy hair.

"Grandmother, tell me a
story," begged the girl.

"To be sure," said Nguyen.
"Wilt thou do nothing with thy
lazy fingers ? "

"I will count the crackers,
grandmother, and I will bring
thee lots of fish to-morrow. Tell
me a story, grandmother ! "

"Ah, child, that is an idle
promise. Shall I tell thee about
the Chinese princess, or of the
good spirit by the riverside ? "

"No, tell me about the brown
maid and the earthworm."

And Nguyen told her tale
there by the smoking wick of
the tiny lamp. The flame
flickered about and shed a gleam

of light here on a pewter vessel,
there in Banh's dark eyes and on
her teeth, and again on a bit of
red paper, and yonder on a patch
of moisture on the mud-built
wall, peopling the dark corners
with hideous reptiles and the air
with flying monsters till Banh's
great frightened eyes fancied
they could see the glimmer of
the earthworm's scales. When
it came to where the monster
eats the maiden she creeps close
to her grandmother.

" The lamp is gone out," said
Nguyen ; " it is time we went to
sleep. Child, put the jar out,
for I think it will rain this night.
Dost thou hear the wild geese ? "

"Grandmother, I dare not stir.
I will sit here till thou comest
back."

Nguyen laughed, and went to
put the jar under the corner of
the hut, so that it might catch
the rain-water running from the
roof. But Banh, too frightened
to remain alone, followed her,
and looking up to the moon

astride on a fluffy cloud, she said—

" Grandmother, when thou didst marry Dinh my grand-father, was he beautiful, and didst thou love him ? "

Nguyen laughed till the tears came to her eyes.

" Thy grandfather was not beautiful, but I did love him. We were young."

" Grandmother, if I do wed any man he must be beautiful. Even as fair as the one who kissed the brown maid."

" Well," said Nguyen, shut-ting the door for the night, " then thou mayst wait a year and a day."

Hardly anybody comes to the little Doson Hotel in the winter; perhaps now and again a solitary wanderer who brings his own provisions and eats them under the deserted, sand-filled veran-dah. Maybe, if he be one of the lucky ones, he will find the hotel open, its mistress having

come from Haiphong to give
the house an airing. Then he
will have a cheery greeting, the
run of the house, and a *bouille-
abaisse* for his dinner.

George Félix was one of these
lucky ones. Good things came
to him overnight. "*Tiens !*" he
said, as he made for the well-
known verandah, " I thought
there was never a soul here in
December, but the door is open."

He proceeded at once on a
tour of inspection, and in one of
the bedrooms came across the
mistress and her boy busy turning over mattresses, and making
things generally unpleasant for
mosquitoes and cockroaches.
After satisfactory arrangements
for a meal in the course of an
hour or two, George Félix went
back to the verandah, pulled out
a shabby, weather-beaten old
long chair, and settled down
comfortably. The shimmering,
noisy sea to the left, the cool,
brick-floored hall to the right.
Comfort spread from the top of

his head to the very tips of his toes, and presently he dreamt a strange dream.

He saw enter into the hall a young Annamite girl as brown as a berry, straight-limbed and slight, carrying under her arm a small empty basket. Looking round, she paused, surprised, before a big looking-glass hung over a dresser. She stood and looked. The girl in the glass did the same. For quite five minutes the two girls were wrapt one in the other. Then the one that was not in the looking-glass said to the other one, " Thou art the brown maid." And they looked again. A noise from the verandah made her turn her head.

Her eyes opened very wide. She stood still awhile, and then came closer to the chair, slowly, step by step, without taking off her eyes from the face of the dreamer. Quite close to the chair she paused. Gently bending on her knees, she leant for-

ward a little and peeped under
the half-closed eyelids, and, speak-
ing to herself, she said, " Thou
art the fair one who kissed the
brown maid."

George Félix did nothing of
the kind, but, opening wide his
fine pair of grey blue eyes, he
stared at the little sunburnt
damsel in blank astonishment.
If Banh had not been Banh she
would have run away at this
propitious moment, but being
the girl she was, and having just
then for the first time in her life
gazed into a bevel-edged looking-
glass, and on the face of a
European, she stayed.

The " fair one " in the long
chair spoke in a soft tongue, and
this is what he said—" *Ma foi !*
she is not at all bad, this little
one. I wonder what she is
looking at me like that for ? "

And Banh thought, " He talks
like music. His hands are as
white as his face. Banh will
go with him." She told him
this first with her lips, and

George Félix did not understand,
later with her eyes, and, reading
easily their simple language, he
paused perplexed.

He did fight a short, unsatis-
factory battle with himself, but,
growing more and more awake
to the delicious novelty of his
adventure, he turned a deaf ear
to reason, and, throwing prudence
to the winds, he laid his hand on
the girl's head, and said, "Come."
And Banh followed him.

That night there were no fish
for the evening meal. Nguyen,
shading her eyes with her hand,
looked long across the paddy-
field. The other children had
come back, the old men too,
and just now the black dog, but
Banh did not come.

Then the old woman sat down
and ate. Often the girl had been
late; she was ever wayward.
But when Nguyen had lit her
lamp, and the mist lay heavy in
the fields, and the country all
around was dark, Nguyen thought,

" I fear something has happened. If she be not with Beo-ben where shall I look for her ? "

Taking her stick, she went out, across the small patches of garden stuff, feeling her way with the stick. As she passed the cottages she could hear the voices within, and the dogs growled. In the high-street she paused before a brick-built house of narrow frontage. The door was already fastened. She knocked, and somebody came to open. She entered a square apartment. Opposite the door, in the place of honour, the family *tablettes*, a small lamp to the left. To the right a passage, through which Nguyen followed the coolie to whom she made her request that she wanted to speak to Beo-ben at once. They went through three more rooms, and then entered another square apartment, where two old men, an old woman, Beo-ben the mistress of the house, and Han her son, sat at meat.

Nguyen saluted the company, and begged them to forgive her intrusion. Then she told Beoben that her grandchild had not come home, and how she thought that the old man might know where Banh was. Beo-ben requested Nguyen to be seated, and sent the coolie to inquire from the old man to whom Beoben gave a daily meal with her servants if he knew anything of the girl.

"No, he knew nothing, and did not remember having seen Banh on the beach."

Then old Nguyen's face grew very grave.

"Good mother," said Han, who had listened in silence, "I will go out on the road with lamps. Fear not, I will bring her back."

Nguyen returned to her cottage, and Han was as good as his word. He and his coolies went on to Doson, searched the beach, every little tuft of seaweed, but they did not find Banh.

And old Nguyen, left all alone, cried night and day.

That was in the first days of December.

But time goes by so quickly, and the good people in the village were beginning to look to the graves of their dead ones, and were busily preparing for the festivities of the New Year.

At the time of the " *Têt* " it always rains — a small, chilly drizzle, penetrating everything.

The green bamboo had been planted in the courtyard at the back of the cottages to invite the departed spirits to come and share the good things. In front, too, the long poles at the top, with branches of foliage and wreathed round with sika leaves, had been fixed.

In Beo-ben's household the festivities of the *Têt* were marred by secret sorrow. Han, the young master, was ill. Something was always ailing him. The doctor, the sorcerer, all had been consulted, but to no good.

There was one who knew where lay the secret source of his failing health, and that was his mother. Since Banh had disappeared from the village, Han, her son, had sickened.

It was the first day of the *Têt*. Volleys of crackers were fired continuously. And it rained a steady drizzle. The villagers, behind their closed doors, each family complete, all absent members drawn together round the festive board, were feasting. And they would feast for three days, three meals and offerings to the dead, and on the door-sills they had painted signs to keep away the bad spirits.

On the embankments between the fields the peasants, in gaily-coloured holiday clothes, come and go: some to town to the theatres, others to distant villages to see their friends.

Beo-ben's house was full of people. The old folks and the mistress were busy entertaining their friends. Servants flushed

with wine, generously provided
for everybody, run hither and
thither with trays heavily laden
with rice and cooked meats and
fishes and sugar dainties. It is
one continual feasting. Even
Thuoc, the old man in clean
clothes, was made use of.

Han, shivering and looking
white and thin, lay on a couch.

"Master," said Thuoc, as he
passed the couch on one occasion, "has the master not heard
that Banh has come back to her
grandmother's house?"

"Thou dost dream, old man,
or hast thou been taking too
much wine?"

"No, no, my master; but I
saw her with my own eyes as I
was carrying thy presents to the
schoolmaster. Just as I was
coming back I saw some one go
into Nguyen's cottage. 'Nguyen,
ha!' I called. But Banh turned
round. She did not answer,
but went inside and shut the
door."

"Mother, didst thou hear what

Thuoc was saying ?   Banh has
come back."

It was the first time this name
was mentioned between mother
and son.

Beo-ben's face grew very pale.
Beo-ben was a proud woman.
The daughter of wealthy parents,
she had married a well-to-do
husband, and had come a very
young wife to the village. Deeply
religious, her everyday life was
interwoven to its very details
with the things of the other
world ; she tended her dead ancestors night and morning with
her own hands ; the caring for
the old people around her was
her very religion and greatest
solicitude. Early she taught her
children to regard the white heads
in their home as emblems of
holiness. Happy and active in
her own household, she had ever
taken an interest in the affairs of
the village. The beggars fed in
her kitchen, and the sick ones
blessed Beo-ben.

Nguyen's husband had been a

distiller of rice alcohol. He had
sold his products to Hanoï, Beo-
ben's husband, who had large
pig-farms.

The people in Nguyen's cottage
were hard-working, honest folks,
but the Evil One had cast an eye
on them, and they were never
prosperous. The men-folk died
early. Nguyen's children married
poorly and away from their native
village, so that when Nguyen
was getting old she was left
alone with Banh, her grand-
daughter. But for a regular,
small remittance from Thiba, her
sister's child, she would have
been poor indeed. Both women
lost their husbands at the same
time, and it is then that Beo-ben
came forth and helped Nguyen
in a hundred ways.

Banh was spoilt. The prettiest
child in the village, she had even
as a baby reigned supreme and
done just as she pleased.

Beo-ben, who had had only
boys herself, had a great love for
the bright, sharp-tongued thing.

Her own boys were quiet, fond of study, and somewhat shy. When the elder ones had married and settled in neighbouring villages, Han, her youngest son, grew even more silent.

Banh came often to play with the boy, and many times she would go and sit in Beo-ben's chamber, and then, putting a needle between the girl's awkward fingers, Beo-ben would teach her how to sew, telling stories in her soft, melodious voice about the good spirits, and how it behoves a young girl to see to the comfort of her parents.

Poor little restless Banh. Five minutes she would hold the needle, unthreading it a dozen times, put in two crooked stitches, and her fingers damp and nervous she would put down the work with a deep sigh.

"Beo-ben," she would say, "but I do love my grandmother, and if I were rich I would give her a fine funeral. I want to play." And running away she would call for Han, and a few minutes later the sound of their laughter would reach to Beo-ben's quiet corner.

But all that had happened long ago. As Beo-ben was standing there so pale before her son, she lived through a moment of bitter anguish. But one word of command would save her from the shame of welcoming as her son's wife a woman who had sinned.

"Han, my son," said Beo-ben, her voice full of deep emotion, "I will go this minute to Nguyen's cottage."

Outside it was already dark. Still it rained, the same little chilly rain. Beo-ben's turned-up slippers splashed in the watery puddles, making echoes everywhere. Merry voices sounded through the doors, lamps were hoisted on the festive poles, and here and there a hasty figure putting a light to a heap of fire-crackers. " Thou shalt wait outside," she said to the coolie who carried her lamp.

Then she knocked at the door, calling out her own name. After awhile the door was opened.

Banh had indeed come back. But not the same Banh who left the village two months ago. There she stood, a sad-faced woman, her clothes besmeared with the mud of the road.

The two women looked at one another in silence.

"Where is my grandmother?" inquired Banh.

"She is gone to live with Thiba, her sister's child. Thiba came here one day when thou wert gone, and she sorrowed when she heard all and saw the loneliness of the old woman, and in the evening made Nguyen go with her. She left the cottage all in readiness. There is food in the cupboard. There is the couch, that if thou shouldst come back thou might have a place where to lay thy head."

Banh turned away her face.

"Come, Banh," continued Beo-ben, "thy clothes are wet. My house is ready. Come with me."

"No," said Banh, looking sadly at Beo-ben, "I must stay here."

Then Beo-ben, thinking of her boy at home, and recalling the anguish of the weeks gone by, told everything.

"Stop, stop, Beo-ben. Thou must tell thy son that Banh can never be any man's wife. Ah! sweet Beo-ben, thou art so dear a mother! I will stay here and tend my sore feet, then will I go and find my old mother."

Beo-ben went home.

"She will not come!" she said to her son, awaiting her return with feverish impatience, and putting her arms round the boy's knees she broke out into passionate weeping.

Han was sinking fast. Each morning found him weaker. There he lay on his couch, dozing in the day, in the night wakeful and burning with fever, sickening at the sight of food. His days were numbered indeed. They said he was dying. His frail body had been carried into the centre chamber of the house according to custom, his face turned to the east. His last weak utterances had been written down, his clothes changed for festive garments, and his hands been laid to his sides. The attendants were preparing to put a bit of cotton-wool under the nostrils, so as to be able to ascertain at once when he would breathe his last, when Beo-ben entered.

The sight of the cotton sent the blood to her heart.

" No, no, not yet. Oh, good spirits, can ye do nothing for my boy ? I will go once more." And casting a long, tender glance at the worn face, she hurried away.

And Beo-ben did plead long and earnestly. At last Banh said, " Well, I will go. But mark ye that, sweet Beo-ben, if thy son be truly dying for love of me, when he will see Banh he will die a hundred deaths."

"Han," said the girl to the boy as they entered, "canst thou see me?"

A wonderful change came over the face. He opened his eyes and said clearly, "Banh, I can see thee."

Turning to those around the girl said, "Go all away, and leave us alone. Thou, too, Beo-ben."

Then, being left with the boy, she came close to his couch, and kneeling by his side she told him a miserable story, and Han cried piteously.

Nobody ever heard the tale but the boy, and when he had heard it he looked into the sad eyes of the bare-footed, half-starved girl, and said in a low voice, "Then thou didst think thy grandmother's fairy tales were true? My little brown maid, ah! I have grieved so much, for

I have loved thee many years. Blessed be the good spirits who brought Banh to Han's home."

When Beo-ben came back she found her son asleep in Banh's arms.

And on the morrow there was feasting and rejoicing in the house of Beo-ben.

And this was the third day of the *Tết*.

www.ingramcontent.com/pod-product-compliance
Lightning Source LLC
Chambersburg PA
CBHW030130030726
47498CB00007B/2642